A... for ASSASSIN

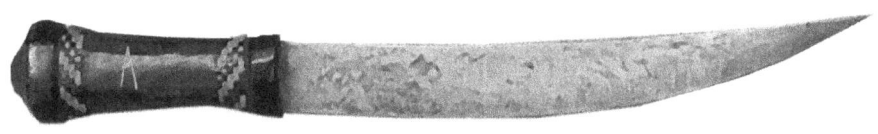

ERNESTO GASTALDI
ENGLISH LANGUAGE TRANSLATION
BY
DAVIDE MANA

RAVEN'S HEAD
PRESS

NEVER SAY NEVERMORE

NEVER SAY NEVERMORE

First Edition • January 2016 • Raven's Head Press • English Language
Copyright © 2016 Ernesto Gastaldi, Michael R. Hudson and Davide Mana
• All rights reserved.

Editor: Michael R. Hudson
Cover Art: Anon

This novella was translated and adapted directly from Ernesto Gastaldi's
original novella "A… come Assassino". We hope you, the reader, will
enjoy the variances from the original as well as from the filmed version.

PUBLISHERS NOTE

Raven's Head Press
Ravensheadpress.com
ISBN-13: 978-0692623930 • ISBN-10: 0692623930

A...For Assassin is an eponymous black comedy play originally titled A... come Assassino by Ernesto Gastaldi. It was the winner of the Premio Istituto Dramma Italiano Award.

In 1966 director Angelo Dorigo directed a film version produced by Walter Brandi based off of the play.

The play is currently in its second edition in Italy. The Raven's Head Press edition has been translated into a novella by author Davide Mana. It is the first English translation of the work.

A... for ASSASSIN

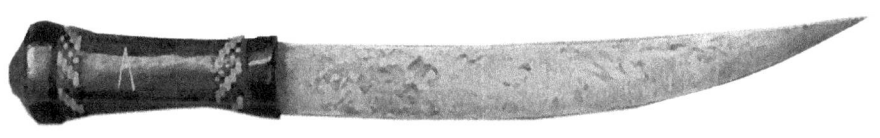

ERNESTO GASTALDI
ENGLISH LANGUAGE TRANSLATION
BY
DAVIDE MANA

CHAPTER ONE

A woman's legs, elegantly stockinged, walk swiftly on the muddy lane leading to John Prescott's villa. Blue lightning is mirrored in the puddles and thunder growls softly, far away. Gusts of wind shake the tops of the trees. The woman stops in front of the gate to the villa. A dog on a chain barks.

The woman shushes it.

"Easy, Bubi!"

A light flicks on in the guardian's bungalow and an ageless man comes out, carrying a flashlight. He illuminates the woman's face. She's in her mid twenties, with copper hair that cascades down over her shoulders. She has the body of a runway model.

The man hastily opens the gate and greets her with a bow: "Miss Angela, welcome back..."

The woman greets him back with a nod and walks towards the black majestic shape of the villa, standing at the end of the grounds, against the clearing sky. A quarter moon's light filters through the dark clouds. Angela turns.

"Ah, Mortimer, leave the gate open. Our car broke down, and Armand took it to the mechanic. He'll be late. What's the time?"

"Well past midnight, miss," the watchman replies.

Angela nods and starts again towards the villa, walking by the white stone edge framing the flowerbeds. Beyond the edges, brushes of heather grow wild and thick, waving with each gust of wind.

The woman climbs the few steps to the ground floor of the house and opens one of the great front French doors. She enters, without switching on the lights, the decision of one that knows the place well. She crosses the hall and climbs up the twin-winged marble staircase, then walks along a wide hallway. Nine lavishly paneled doors open onto the corridor.

The lights are off, but the hallway is not dark: the moonlight filters through the frosted glass of a skylight, following the rhythms of the running clouds. In the brightest moments, the moonlight shines on the weapon panoplies hanging on the walls: samurai swords, Indonesian daggers, and medieval broadswords.

As Angela passes by, a door moves. The brass doorknob turns, without any noise, and a door inches open silently. Then, as slowly as it opened, it closes again. Angela is alerted by a sixth sense, and feeling observed she turns in time to see the door close. She stops and listens: the wind in the chimneys takes on the wailing tone of human voices. Angela sighs and moves along. She passes two more closed doors. Behind her, the creak of hinges needing oil announces a second check from somebody, but the woman does not turn to watch anymore. She stops in front of the seventh door, her room. But a blade of light marks the closed door. It comes from around the corner in the hallway. Out of curiosity she goes and checks: the ninth door, the one leading to the study of John Prescott, her uncle, is barely open. Angela approaches the door and peeps in, but the crack is too narrow to see within. She tarries a moment, and then knocks.

"Uncle John!" she calls, but there's no answer.

Angela opens the door wide to see John Prescott, as he lay sprawled in his leather chair, an arm hanging loosely on one side, his head on the desktop. His eyes are gazing, a look of surprise on his face. Stuck in his ripped-open throat there's a weird-looking dagger. A big, ornately gothic "A" is etched on the wooden handle. From his carotid, neatly severed, much blood has dripped, drenching his blue silk smoking jacket. The old man's mouth is open, exposing his gold molar teeth and his curled up, blackened tongue. Behind him, an imposing safe is similarly open, two rows of gold Sterling coins mimicking and mocking the dead master's mouth.

Angela screams.

CHAPTER TWO

YORKSHIRE EVENING POST
Slain in his villa billionaire John Prescott
THE GUARDIAN
All guilty or none guilty: who has slain Mr. Prescott?
THE TIMES
The murder of Leeds
The police groping in the dark: all are suspects.

Full-page headlines run on local and national newspapers. The homicide brings back the character of John Prescott, exceedingly well known in the City, despite his desertion, in the last two years, of London and its clubs, as he retired in his huge mansion in West Yorkshire.

The papers hint at unsavory stories, at a dark past in South Africa, where he arrived penniless and from which he came back a billionaire. There are innuendos at 'liaisons dangereuses' between the old man and all of the females in his family. Those papers that have photos publish them, teasing the readers' curiosity with colorful pages on the inhabitants of Prescott's villa, trying to uncover who, amongst them, might be the one that cut the old man's throat.

On the other hand, the newspapers closest to the victim's interest lament the death of a pillar of British society. The killing, they say, must be the act of a robber, one skilled enough to bypass all the physical obstacles and the electronic security systems of the villa.

The police state that every option was evaluated and investigated. For security reasons, the investigators have the whole of Prescott's family under house arrest, including the servants, but to the newspapers this translates as "the Police are out of their depth".

The sales of scandal-mongering tabloids peak: one shows a photo of Angela, the victim's youngest niece, in a swimsuit so tiny it looks like a dental floss ad, and chatters about her socialite life as well as her sexual preferences. Among those in line who have enjoyed Angela in her bed, the prospective winner is Armand, a distant cousin, and free-climbing champion. He's got a poster-boy physique, more popular with horny males than women.

There are photos of another beauty living at the villa, Audrey, wife of George, one of John Prescott's nephews. She's less classy than Angela, she's also more physically endowed and sexy as hell. One of the photos is a freeze-frame of an acrobatic dance twirl, caught in the Speed Queen nightclub, in Leeds. The caption poses a fundamental question: does the niece of the dead billionaire ever wear panties?

At Prescott's funeral there's a lot of people watching, but few follow the hearse to the gravesite. None of the relatives living at the villa asked to be there. Only Jack, the fiftyish butler, companion in some of the most unsavory adventures of the old man, asked for a leave to attend. But the Inspector's decision has been unmoved: nobody can leave the villa, without exception.

On the first page of the Yorkshire Evening Post there's a photo of a middle-aged woman, all in black, wearing a large medallion. She's not Prescott's widow, the old rake never married. She's his sister, the widow of Burton Prescott. Her name is Marta Prescott. The newspaper wonders about the final destination of the victim's riches. The name of the heir (or heirs) might be a lead to identify the murderer. It is the usual 'cui prodest', since the times of the dramatist Seneca that is teasing the investigators, including the police official assigned to handle the case, Inspector Walter Brand. Who profits?

Prescott never had a wife and yet he has a son, Julian. Mother unknown. John brought him back from an African adventure, together with cartloads of diamonds. The mother had died in childbirth, John had said. A son born out of incest, the backbiters insinuated.

Julian is sixteen but his mental age is that of a seven-year-old child. The nastiest gossips speak of syphilis on his father's side, the kinder ones hint at childhood trauma. The only one taking care of him, like he was her own son, is Marta, who's been mourning her husband since he died in Africa, twenty years ago.

Another dark story, that one. A violent death, a stab in the throat. The killer was never identified. The motive never known.

Marta, after the tragedy, returned to Yorkshire, where her sister Sheena, a widow, was raising two small children. She too had come home with a bag of diamonds, but much smaller than her brother's, who had spent two more years in Africa than she had.

Her sister, Sheena suffered from plaque sclerosis and died a few months after Marta's arrival. Marta had taken care of her two nephews, but she'd never been able to establish a loving, trusting relationship with them. She was too wrapped up in her own pain, gnawed by a suspicion she has never revealed to anyone.

Angela and George were nine and eleven respectively, when John Prescott had returned as a billionaire from Africa with one-year old Julian. The child was learning to crawl, and he was beautiful, blond-haired, smiling, and seemingly normal.

Knighted by the Queen, Sir John had bought the great mansion just outside of Leeds and reunited the broken wreckage of his family. Included in the price of the mansion was Mortimer, the guardian watchman that lives in the outbuilding studio by the grounds gate: he was staying there when Lord Philip had bought the house that he later sold to Sir John Prescott. Mortimer's age was impossible to gauge, just like the mansion's, which was part Baroque, part Victorian.

Three days after Prescott's funeral, the estate executor, Sedwick, enters the great hall of the mansion, together with Inspector Brand along with two uniformed officers that are there in case they are needed.

Brand is a grizzled man, close to his pension, the pockets of his pied de poule jacket sagging for usage, his fulled woolen pants are worn at the knees.

The attorney, Sedwick, is a thin man, his skin textured like parchment, all in gray down to his spats. A middle-aged office boy, hot on his heels, carries a black leather bag that draws the greedy glances of the prospective heirs, sitting in a half-circle in front of the great oval dining table.

Everybody stands up and Brand gestures for them to sit.

"My name is Walter Brand, Inspector Walter Brand. We've met already in Park Street. And this is Mr. Sedwick, who Sir John nominated as executor of his last will and testament."

Jack, the butler, in his formal pinstripe jacket, pours tea in the cups of the future heirs. As he pours, he murmurs ironically, "The tea is ready and…" and he nods towards the executor, "dinner will be served soon sir."

Brand does not smile and points the butler to an empty chair, at the far end of the half-circle. Jack sits down and turns to Marta.

"Excuse me, madam, if I sit by your side. The Law commands me." Marta looks at him without really seeing him, as ladies used to do with servants. She strokes one of Julian's hands. The boy whines, "Aunt Marta, tea gives me the runs..."

Marta shushes the boy with a smile. "Don't say things like that," she whispers.

"Yes Aunt Marta, but tea causes me..."

Marta mercifully places her hand over the mouth of the youth and shakes her head with maternal affection. Julian hangs his head, and then kisses her hand. Marta's eyes fill with tears.

"Someone is missing," the Inspector says dryly. They all look at each other and then stare at Brand, uncomprehending.

The Inspector counts them.

"One, two, three, four, five, six, seven! There should be eight. Who's missing?"

Nobody answers, and then Julian, in a querulous childish voice starts chanting.

"Mortimer's missing, Mortimer's missing, Mortimer's missing!"

"Uh, Mortimer..." Marta breathes.

"What's the old watchman got to do with all this, Inspector? He's not family!" George huffs, while arranging a blond wisp of hair that has fallen across his narrow forehead.

His wife, Audrey, sits by his side, irrepressible in a low cut cardinal red dress that barely contains her enormous tits. She arranges the lace of the kerchief in her husband's breast pocket with a dainty gesture and smiles demurely at him. "He's not family but he is a part of the household, isn't he?" she intones.

"More than that, Uncle bought him with the house," Angela says. "Jack's not family either, after all." Handsome Armand glances ironically to the butler who nods in agreement but does not reply to the derisive remark thrown his way.

While the attorney's assistant sets the table, extracting papers and files from the bag, one of the uniformed men calls Mortimer to join the others. The attorney sits down, straightens the files, with professional precision, while tension and impatience rise among the heirs. As he waits, he clears his throat and then stares at the great oil painting hanging on the salon's wall: it's John Prescott, looking down with grim but sardonic eyes at the not-so-happy crew waiting to split his riches.

"It's like Sir John was here too," Sedwick says, not a line moving in his dried-up face as his eyes gaze upon the huge oil painting.

Julian turns to the painting. "What's up, father?" the boy exclaims.

Marta gestures for him to be silent and then adds, "He's watching us," she whispers, "from the sky."

Armand hears her and grins. "Or from Hell..."

No one makes further comments because Mortimer enters the room, looking embarrassed with his cap in hand. Brand has another chair brought in. Now there's eight of them waiting for the will to be opened.

The attorney begins with a simple, comprehensive gesture.

"We are hereby reunited to listen to the last will and testament of Sir John Prescott, who left us so suddenly and violently. His horrible death still oppresses me…"

Angela sighs and crosses her legs. The two uniformed cops can't help but stare.

"Read, Mr. Sedwick!" George orders, impatiently.

Sedwick glances at him, dispassionate but scolding, then something like a smile crosses his parchment-like face, yes, the Inspector is certain of the murderer he thought, and his eyes flash irony for a brief moment.

"I will not need to read, ladies and gentlemen. You will listen to the last will of Sir John directly from his own living voice."

"Living?" Julian asks. Marta strokes his head praying for the boy to be silent. The youth shrugs and jumps off his chair.

Marta stands suddenly, and the Inspector huffs. "What now?"

Julian looks intimidated and lifts two fingers in a V sign.

"I need to pee, mister teacher sir."

"Just throw that poor idiot out..." Audrey spits.

The Inspector gestures for Marta to go with Julian, who walks with both hands covering his crotch, and then bursts out in singsong laughing without any visible reason.

"We all look like good people, Inspector," Angela smiles, "and yet you think one of us is a murderer."

The Inspector bends his head halfway, in a manner that means neither yes nor no.

"I don't think," he says. "I'm paid to observe and piece together the facts. You arrived at midnight and found your uncle with his throat cut."

Angela nods, and the Inspector continues.

"So you say. You say you arrived at midnight and found your uncle with his throat cut," he repeats.

15

Angela smiles, amused. Sarcastically she adds, "Ah but Mortimer, the watchman, *says* it too."

"That's true. Mortimer says your claim is true." Brand stresses the word 'says', and then turns to Mortimer. "What's your pay?"

"Nine thousand pounds a year, plus lodging."

"Too low a figure to fit into a homicide case."

"Rightly so, sir, " the watchman replies punctiliously.

"And I arrived forty minutes later," Armand says, enjoying his interruption. "The ambulance was here already, and it was useless. Therefore I'm in the clear of this sordid mess."

The Inspector nods. "This also is true. Mortimer *says* you came back at twelve forty. The killing took place between ten and eleven pm, so you had ample time to leave and come back."

Armand, who was nodding in time with the Inspector, a smug smile on his face, suddenly stops and looks at him askew.

Meanwhile, the attorney has picked up a padded envelope, sealed with wax. He opens it, and extracts a tape recorder. He places it on the table and glances at the Inspector, his finger at ready on the play button.

Brand shakes his head. They have to wait for Marta and Julian to come back.

Angela uncrosses her legs, and puffing out her tits, catches the two cops staring, and smiles. Jack stands and picks up the great teapot.

"Sir, a spot of tea?" he asks the attorney.

"Thanks. I don't drink on the job," the attorney replies.

Angela and Armand trade a glance, and they chuckle with complicity.

Julian comes back, together with Marta. Julian sniffs his hands, and then puts his fingers in his mouth with a look of total bliss in his eyes. Audrey looks the other way. "Disgusting!" she whispers to her husband.

George nods in agreement.

When everyone is sitting in their place again, Sedwick's finger brushes the play button but stops.

"Please, ladies and gentlemen, do not interrupt Sir John's last speech."

Angela quips, "Nobody ever interrupted John Prescott, come on and play the damned thing!"

Sedwick casts a lackluster but stern look at Angela, and presses play.

A hiss, and then a male voice, deep, warm but authoritarian, a voice charged with charisma, a voice that inspires obedience begins to speak.

"Good evening. I am John Prescott. Better, I was John Prescott, but right now I still am. Therefore I was, speaking of the future. Funny, eh? It's like there was no present." Audrey sighs and looks at the ceiling. *As if he was able to see her, Prescott's voice adds "Audrey, dear, don't be impatient. You have to allow a poor dead man a little bit of after-dinner philosophizing."*

Audrey freezes and is about to speak, but the executor stops her with a gesture, and points to the big oil painting. "Shush," he says. "He knows, or rather he knew."

Marta and Angela cast an involuntary glance at the painting from which Prescott seems to be laughing down at them.

The recorded voice continues.

"I see you all around the table, knives and forks in hand, dribbling with anticipation. Nice word, dribbling, unusual word too. Had I said that saliva is falling from your mouths it would have been vulgar. But one thing is certain: none of you are worthy of my money."

The voice stops and the hiss of static sounds like the end of the tape. Audrey, George and Angela stand up, but the attorney gestures for them to sit down. They comply slowly. After a few seconds, the voice starts up again, in a sarcastic tone.

"I bet that Audrey, George and Angela stood, aghast, thinking it was the end of my will. Marta instead remained seated, and my old friend Jack too, sure, and Mortimer, who would stand only if commanded so. As for my son Julian I don't know, crazies are unpredictable..."

Julian grins. "Crazy, crazy..." he repeats. "Father always called me crazy... Aunt Marta, am I crazy?"

Marta shakes her head and gestures for him to be silent.

"... and then there's Armand, who says he's the son of the stepdaughter of the stepsister of my mother. He says he's here because he's screwing Angela, but I know he's aiming at something else."

Armand gestures in protest, but Angela quiets him placing a hand on his arm.

Audrey grins and whispers, "That pig doesn't play around with words."

"Don't make those faces," John Prescott says. *"Let's call fuck for what it is. I'm sorry Marta."* The woman lowers her eyes and sighs in resignation.

17

"... your Arthur, too, could not stand such vulgarities, but in the end they are the only words that seem to hold meaning."

Marta places her hand over the locket she wears on her neck, as John continues, *"Marta, your Arthur was flavorless and boring like one of your puddings. I never told you, little sister, but that was always my opinion and I could never understand why his death was to you not a liberation but a malady."* A coughs, and then the voice starts again. *"Sorry...Dr. McCorney says too many cigars, but I am sure it won't be smoking that will kill me. I've had a good life: I was dishonest without regrets; I corrupted, whored, raped without misgivings: if everything past is lost, as they say, I passed up very little."* He chuckles. *"Even those bitches who said they would not, in the end, were quite willing. So now my problem is not moral, when I ask myself: to whom will I leave all this money? It's just a matter of choice, made bitter by the fact that I'm now out of the game of life. And such a fantastic game it was that really killed me. Yes, killed me. I hope you are still there, all of you: my son Julian, my sister Marta, my nephews Angela and George, my daughter-in-law Audrey, my momentary son-in-law Armand, old Jack and Mortimer, too."*

Mortimer is the only one that bends forward, bowing in response to the voice on the recorder.

"All right, you are all here. I'll propose you a game. And you will need to listen well: everything I own will go to only three of you. Only three of you have the opportunity of getting filthy rich. But who will the three be? The three of you, male or female I don't care, relatives, in-laws or servants, you are all on the same starting line, with equal opportunities. Three of you, I was saying, in one month will meet here with my attorney to cash in their inheritance. If only two show up, they'll share my patrimony fifty/fifty. Should only one be here, he or she will get the entire lot. Should nobody show up, everything will go to the Foundation for the Redemption of Lost Girls. You, Mortimer, are not in the game. To you I leave Bubi, the dog, who's the only one that really loved me in the end."

George is the first to protest. "If this is a joke, Sedwick, it's in extreme bad taste."

"George, shut up," Marta sighs. "It's an invitation to break the law. My brother was like that."

The attorney asks for silence with an imperious gesture and the recorded voice starts speaking once again. The words of Prescott miraculously seem to be responding to Marta's retort.

"Why do you call my proposal an invitation to break the law? Considering the harmony and lack of self-interest that seem to govern our family, you will need to

somehow find an accord and choose three to inherit, and they will generously share the lot with you. Each one of you wanted me dead and I am, but I do not know why I died, how I died, and where I died. This means I can't send you my love: some one of you might have cut the thread of the Norns before it was time. So to you I simply say, have a good life, as long as you can."

Julian's petulant voice is the first to break the silence. "The Norns? Were the Norns normal, Aunt Marta?"

The would-be heirs trade glances loaded with questions and diffidence. Marta stands and takes Julian by the hand.

"I have no interest in my brother's money, but I do have to think about Julian's welfare."

"And not ours, Auntie? Our mother was also a sister of Uncle John." Angela shakes her golden halo of hair. "And she was also a shareholder in the African diamond society, right?" Marta stiffens.

"I'm sure you can perfectly well take care of your concerns on your own."

Audrey stands, furious. "George. Don't let these people screw you. You have to be one of the three that will be here for the inheritance."

George nods without any enthusiasm. "Sure, darling, sure. But right now I need a breath of fresh air.

"One moment, ladies and gentlemen, please," says the Inspector. And then to the attorney, "Are you finished?"

"For the moment, yes," Sedwick replies. "I will see you in a month."

The Inspector nods.

"Maybe. You can go." He turns to the others. "You can't. I'd like to recap your affidavits."

George huffs. "Again! We already gave our statements in Park Street, they took our fingerprints and wrote everything down."

"But now I am in charge of the case, and I love hearing statements live."

"What else do you need to know, Inspector," Angela asks, giving him her child-like stare, the one that always defused any suspicion. "You've already tortured us in every way possible."

Brand smiles back sympathetically, and pulls out a notebook. "Old style..." he says. "I need to write it down with my pen or I can't remember. So: somebody cut the throat of Sir John Prescott between ten and eleven pm. We know because the safe had a timer, and it was opened only within that time frame." He stares at them. "Does anyone among you know the safe code?"

Nobody answers. Then Julian cackles.

"The code of the safe is the key of it all. It's safe to say that!" says Brand.

"Eh eh eh..."

The way Julian laughs makes everyone uneasy. His laughter sounds metallic, and its tone gets lower, turning into a dribbled mumble that ends with an evil hum.

The Inspector glances at him and then turns to Marta.

"Is this young man always like this?"

Audrey grins. "Only on Sundays. What a silly question, Inspector? He was born like that!"

"Eh eh eh..." Julian chuckles in reply. He crouches down by Marta's feet, and she ruffles his hair and says, "He was not born like this. Somebody did something to him, when he was still a child."

The Inspector pulls out a folder and spreads some photos on the table. They show Sir John, the dagger sticking in his neck, spread-eagled on the desk. The whole scene has been photographed,

and the details blown up.

Angela browses through the photographs as Inspector Brand tries to summarize the situation.

"I'll ask a quick round of questions to determine what you were doing and where you were at the time of the homicide. But first a question for you all: has anybody ever seen that dagger before the killing?" He picks up a photo showing in detail the murder weapon stuck in the victim's neck. "... And there's no doubt this was the killer weapon..."

"Are you joking, Inspector?" Audrey asks.

Brand sighs. "Spending lots of time among killers and corpses makes one cynical. Well, then, it's obvious this dagger with an 'A' does belong to someone."

They all shake their heads. Mortimer gets really close to the photo to see it better and then adds, "Never saw it," he says.

"So this is nothing that Sir John kept on his desk and the killer may have used on impulse."

Nobody answers.

"Time, now. Each one of you please tell me exactly what you were doing the night of the murder. Where you were, etcetera. Let's start with you, miss...?"

"Angela."

"Miss Angela."

"As you can read in my deposition, I found my uncle's body. I was coming home after the theater, it was midnight."

"You alone?"

"Yes. I had been to theater with Armand, but the car had some problems and he said it only ran on three cylinders, so I did the last stretch on foot, while Armand brought the car to the mechanic."

"At midnight...?" Brand asks.

Armand butts in. "Yes, you can check. The mechanic is a friend of mine, we are both into vintage cars."

Brand writes down in his notes and glances at Angela, waiting for her to continue.

"I was greeted by Mortimer, and I went upstairs to my room. I saw a light on in my uncle's office and I went to take a look, and ... well, I found that." She points at a photo. "I started screaming, and somebody called the police."

"Who?"

"I did," Marta answers. "I called."

"The police, not an ambulance?" Brand asks.

Marta looks embarrassed for a moment.

"Well, it was pretty obvious he was dead."

"Yes. Obvious. The medical examiner says..." He rummages in his pockets and extracts some crumpled sheets. "... that he was killed between eleven and eleven thirty, but considering the quick loss of blood, the murder could also have taken place around midnight. The safe has a timer, right?"

"Yes, it can be only opened only between ten and ten-thirty."

"But it could have been left open for hours, right?"

"Yes," Marta whispers.

"So, if only Sir John knew the combination," the Inspector thinks out aloud, studying the faces of the family members, "this tells us the murder could not have been committed before ten, but after that, it does not tell us anything."

"Your turn, miss...?"

"Audrey, I'm the wife of George Prescott."

George nods and hugs his wife.

"My wife, Inspector. I am... I was Sir John's nephew."

"Fine. Miss Audrey, where were you and what did you do on the night of the homicide?"

"We were in our room, my husband and me. We had been watching the TV in the salon until about nine. Marta and Julian had been there too. She was trying to amuse the retard with a game of solitaire..."

Julian smiles. "The solitaire did not work out," he starts repeating, "It did not work out, remember Aunt Marta, it did not work out."

The Inspector glances at Marta, who nods and says, "We played cards for a while, then I put Julian to bed and went to my room."

Inspector Brand moves on to interrogating George.

"Do you confirm all this? You went to bed at nine o'clock and did not leave the room afterwards?"

George has a brief hesitation that the Inspector does not fail to notice.

"Yes. We were awakened by Angela's screams after midnight."

The Inspector grimaces but nods, thinks for a while, and then turns to the butler.

"You are?"

"Jacques de Volleroy, but everybody calls me Jack. I've been with Sir John since the time of Africa, back then Mr. Prescott was not yet a knight and I had lost my title of count. Then, you know how life goes, we traded places."

Angela seems surprised. "But really Jack, you're a count?"

"At your service, Miss Angela," Jack grins, with a little courtesy.

"You know. Jack," Angela goes on, "as a butler I always found you too, how can I say, too noble. You serve without being the slightest bit servile."

"You're too good, miss," Jack says bowing his head.

Inspector Brand interrupts their little dance. Audrey huffs and crosses her legs deliberately, glancing at the two young cops at the back of the hall, to see if she's being as successful as Angela was before. She smiles meeting their appreciative stares.

"And you, Count Jack, where were you the night of the crime, between ten and midnight?"

Jack stares the Inspector in the eye. "At about ten," he replies easily, "I went to Sir John's office to see if he still needed me. He said he did not, so I went to the kitchen to fix myself a cup of tea. Then, about twenty minutes later, I came here to the salon to wish goodnight to Miss Marta, who was playing cards. She gave me permission to retire, so I went to my room, in the attic, and went to bed. I too was awakened by the screams of Miss Angela. I ran downstairs and ... I saw John ... Sir John ... my master, but also an old friend, with that knife in his throat. I felt it in my throat, too..."

"Jack, when you said goodnight to Sir John, was the safe open or closed?"

"Closed, Inspector."

"Was Sir John in the habit of leaving the safe open for long periods of time?"

"No, Inspector. John ... Sir John was very proud of the fact that nobody, himself included, could open the safe outside of the set time, and he rarely opened it, shutting it as soon as possible."

The Inspector paces up and down, and then asks, "Did you all know the safe opening time?"

George speaks up, irritated. "Yes, Inspector Brand, yes. Uncle used to boast about it, and I think he locked himself up in his office before he opened it. I never saw it open."

"Ah! Did anyone ever see it open?"

Angela nods. "I did. One night Uncle John wanted to show me some diamonds. He had a bag full, as big as nuts. A wonder."

"Did he give any to you?"

"He offered, but I didn't accept."

"Why?"

Angela laughs. "Because he wanted something in exchange!"

Marta is aghast. "Angela! There's no need to speak evil of the dead!"

"Speak evil? Aunt Marta, everybody here knows he was a lecherous pig, now the Inspector knows too. Don't you agree, Audrey?"

Audrey sighs, stands up, and shrugs. "Yes, he was always trying. Even with that servant, do you remember? She was ugly as sin, but to him... as long as she had a..."

"Stop it!" Marta shouts.

Julian pulls at her sleeve. "What did he try?" he asks petulantly. "What did he try? With the women, what did he try with the women...?"

"Nothing, Julian, nothing. Your father was a good man."

Angela laughs. Audrey looks at Marta with irony written all over her face.

"Okay, let's not speak evil, but also let's not sing praises only because he's dead." She passes a hand through her hair and the Inspector notices a diamond on the ring finger of her right hand. It sparkles the colors of rainbow, set in a thin golden band.

"What was your relationship with your husband's uncle?"

Angela chuckles. Audrey glances sideways at her.

She sits down, crosses and uncrosses her legs, pulls the hem of her skirt, trying unsuccessfully to cover her knees.

"Good," she says tentatively, smiling at her husband.

"Did the old man ever try anything with you...?" the Inspector asks.

George stands up. "Inspector, isn't this beyond the boundaries of good taste?"

"When somebody gets his throat cut, good taste is no longer an issue. Answer my question, miss Audrey."

"But of course, quite often," Audrey admits, and then she smiles. "But never beyond the boundaries of good taste."

"Oh!" the Inspector exclaims. "And what was your answer?"

"Inspector!" George interjects, but Audrey gestures for him to calm down.

"No. I simply replied no. That was always enough."

Brand thinks about it and then nods to himself, following some private line of reasoning. Then he turns to Mortimer.

"Could somebody enter the villa without you noticing?"

Mortimer turns his cap in his hands.

"As far as I can be certain of human things, I'd say no. I've got a dog that barks as soon as he hears something amiss. But the grounds perimeter is rather long."

"Alarm systems?"

"There's an infrared alarm along the perimeter."

"Should anyone cross it, what would happen?"

"The lights go up, an alarm goes off and an automatic call gets to the Park Street department."

"We received no call," said Brand.

Mortimer opens his hand and waves it slightly, to underscore that statement.

"Miss Marta," Brand goes on, "What was your relationship with your brother?"

"A sister's. John never let us want for anything, at least where our material comforts and the house necessities were concerned. He always paid our bills without conditions."

"You mean he kept you all?"

"He wanted us all to stay with him."

"I work for the War Museum," George says proudly, "and I always paid my wife's bills without the need to ask Uncle for money."

"But did you know that your uncle was, so to speak, looking for openings with your wife?"

"But of course not!" Audrey exclaims. "He was just a lecherous old man. I never mentioned it to George. There was no need for it."

"And you were wrong in not doing so, Audrey. Very wrong," George replies punctiliously, but without any anger in his voice.

"Because had she told you, " Brand presses him, "what would have you done?"

"I'd have left this house together with my wife."

"You would have broken up with your uncle?"

"Obviously."

Julian's tinny laugh surprises the Inspector. He looks at the boy and "You are Julian, right?" he asks.

"They call me like that, sometimes," Julian grins, standing up. Marta holds his hand and Julian smiles at her. "Aunt Marta always calls me Julian, the others never."

"And what do they call you?"

Julian doesn't answer. He shrugs.

"They don't call me," he laughs.

"Where were you when your father was killed?"

Brand's question is brutal by design, but Julian does not seem to mind. "I was sleeping, wasn't I, Aunt Marta? Even if you did not tell me the story of the little bird..."

Marta smiles and nods, stroking his hand.

"But of course I told you," she replied to the boy.

"Can you tell it to me, too?" the Inspector asks. Marta stares at him in surprise.

"The fairy tale? You want me to tell you the tale of the little bird?"

"Yes, please."

"My father used to tell it to me before I became stupid," Julian says, in a serious tone. "But when I covered myself in shit he got angry, and since then Aunt Marta tells it to me. Right, Aunt? Right, Aunt? Right, Aunt?"

Julian starts whining without reason, and dries his nose with the back of a hand before inserting one finger up his nose.

"Yes, yes. Be good, Julian." She turns to Brand. "Is this taking much longer, Inspector?"

"I don't know," Brand sighs, and stares at Julian who is wiping his finger on his trousers. "Do you know who killed your father?" he asks him.

Marta's fury is about to explode, but she manages to say nothing. Julian nods energetically.

The Inspector gets closer to the boy who becomes the center of attention. Brand spies their faces, seeing curiosity, some worry, but nobody really seems to be afraid of the revelation the mentally challenged boy might make. Mortimer is no longer turning his cap in his hands; his neck is stretched like a turtle's. Armand and Angela trade a glance, and she shakes her head, as in response to an unexpressed question. George gets closer to Audrey in a protective gesture. The only one that's grinning, sitting in his place, is Jack, the butler.

Julian keeps nodding, his head bobbing up and down, but he does not speak. Brand stops him with two fingers under his chin, forcing him to look up.

"Who?" the Inspector asks.

Julian stares with his tearful blue eyes, then points at Mortimer. "Him."

Mortimer opens his mouth, speechless. But Julian is also pointing at Armand. "Him."

"What the fuck are you making up, you fucking retard?" Armand says, but Julian is pointing at each one in turn.

"Him, her, her, him."

Angela huffs. "Inspector, why are you torturing this poor kid? Really, do you think you'll get something useful? He doesn't know what's he's saying."

Brand is staring at Julian, who is still pointing his finger. Then the youth bends his arm and pushes his finger up his nose again. "Aunt," he whines, "can we go play?"

Marta smiles. ""Now we'll go, Julian, now. What do you want to play with?"

"With the wood chips, Aunt, the wood chips!" Julian cries joyfully, and drags his aunt to the door.

Marta follows him. Brand doesn't say anything, and Julian drags his aunt out of the salon.

"Can we go too, Inspector?" Audrey asks.

Brand nods, and then thinks again. "Can anybody tell me the story of the little bird?"

Angela chuckles. "It's the one with that old moral, half wisdom and half mafia."

"Yes," Armand smiles, "the moral is 'mind your own business'."

The Inspector gestures to Angela, and she starts telling the story.

"One day a little bird fell from his nest. He still could not fly, and down on the ground it was very cold. He twittered loud and desperate. A cow walked by and, splash, dumped a big warm cow pie on him. The little bird, not feeling the cold anymore, twittered even louder, with joy. But that was not a good idea: a wolf heard him, came closer, and with a single stroke of his tongue picked him out of his shit cover and ate him."

The Inspector nods.

"Yes, yes, I know it," he says. "The moral is that not all those that cover you in shit mean to hurt you, and not all those that get you out of the shit mean to help, and if you're in deep shit you better shut up."

"It's as old as the hills," Audrey observes, "but when Julian really covered himself in shit, Sir John got royally pissed off."

"And he did not tell the story anymore."

"No. But Julian kept begging for it, and since then Marta has taken Uncle John's place."

The cell phone rings in Brand's pocket.

"Yes..." he listens for a while. "Ah, everybody's. I want the file on my desk, tomorrow morning." He closes his cell phone and puts it back in his pocket. Then he stares at each of them in turn. "You're a fine band of liars. We found your fingerprints on the murder weapon. Everybody's, except those of Mortimer. It did travel a lot, this dagger nobody ever saw."

Each one of the accused tries to look as innocent as possible. Angela even has an answer. "Inspector, my uncle collected bladed weapons. If there's everybody's fingerprints on it, it's because he probably showed it to us, some time or other, even if I can't remember."

"With an A etched on the hilt. A as in Angela, A as in Audrey, A as in Armand."

Nobody comments but Julian's voice echoes, evil and mocking,

27

from some other room.

"A for Assassin!"

CHAPTER THREE

The fingerprint charts slide on the computer screen, and in a sidebar, a long list of mug shots and names appear.

"See, Walter. Nobody's missing. Oh, yeah, the watchman, but everybody else's here. Old Marta, the house slut with her cuckold husband, the blonde hottie, the boy toy, the butler and the idiot. And yet nobody apparently gripped the knife's handle to strike."

Alan Turing, the white-coated technician, picks up a transparent plastic bag. Sealed within is the big knife with the wooden handle, an A etched in it, the murder weapon.

"You're telling me, Alan, that there's fingerprints from all of my suspects on it, and yet the killer used gloves?"

"Possibly, yes. How did it go with the will as cause?"

"Nothing doing. The old bastard drew such a smartass will, had any one of them known about it; they would never have killed him. Considering the situation in that house, he probably wrote the will that way as a life insurance policy. Anyone doing him in was doing everybody else a favor. But it didn't work, and somebody killed him anyway." Brand takes the evidence bag, and looks at it. "Weird knife. Great blade, and a rough wooden handle."

"Pretty common in sub-Saharan areas. They used to import the blades and fit them with locally-made handles."

"So, it's a knife the old man took home on his way back from Africa?"

Alan shrugs. "He didn't kill himself. His fingerprints are not on the knife."

"No doubt about that, but..." Brand muses on his own words, and Alan laughs, anticipating him.

"But there should be his fingerprints if it was part of his collection."

Brand smiles and points a finger. "See Alan? A little of your great-uncle rubbed off. No cyanide apple today."

Alan laughs. The Inspector turns to go, then stops. "Seeing you're in your genius phase, any hypothesis on this murder?"

Alan shakes his head. "If one of the family cut the old man's throat and now has to deal with the smartass will, to inherit they'll have to kill again. If they do, you might get lucky."

"Mmhh, I see the genius minute's over. Be seeing you, Alan."

Brand turns up his coat collar. The sun is setting and a north wind is coming that freezes the tip of his nose. He turns on Great George and walks in the direction of the Vic, his favorite pub. He needs a beer to clear his head.

Upon entering, he makes a beeline for the bar. The publican doesn't need to ask anything, and places a pint of Geordie Yorkshire in front of him. Brand looks at the fine amber color of the beer, focusing his thoughts. No relative of the old adventurer shows the stuff of a killer. Only two male suspects: George and that weird former-count-now-butler that is probably the only one with the guts to actually slit a man's throat.

"Looking for the killer at the bottom of the glass?" The female voice makes the Inspector jump. He glances at the brunette perched on the stool next to him. Very short hair, early forties, slacks, sweater, and tablet in hand.

"Yeah," Brand replies. "News for your paper."

"That sure beats 'Inspector Walter Brand doesn't understand shit, don't you think?" She nods to the barman. "A Martini, please."

The Inspector downs half his pint, then dries his lips with the back of his hand.

"Listen, Julie, there's something I've got to tell you."

He gestures for her to get closer, and Julie leans towards him. "Write whatever the fuck you please, ok?"

Julie laughs and sips the Martini the barman placed in front of her.

"Black humor, I see. Well, I'll give you a tip. The voice on the street is that the two beauties of the villa … Angela and Audrey, are lesbians, There's a photo around, of them kissing, shot a few years back at the Speed Queen."

Brand drinks the other half of his beer and puts down the empty glass. "The voice on the street is the same about you. Killed anybody?"

Julie shrugs. "Who knows? You're the one paid to find these things out."

Brand climbs down from his stool and says, "Put it on my account," to the barman. "Also this ballbreaker's martini." He turns to

Julie, "Provided she stops breaking them."

"As soon as you know the killer's name..."

"I'll call you, okay?"

Brand leaves and Julie sits alone with her martini.

"A call would be nice..." she mumbles in her glass. "Not just when you want to fuck..."

CHAPTER FOUR

Julian is sitting on the ground in a corner of the salon, tongue out, his total concentration on building unlikely human figures using wood scraps. Marta checks on him from time to time. Jack comes in from a door to the kitchen, pushing a cart with tea and biscuits.

"It's five o clock. And all assassins have tea at five," Julian says out loud, his eyes still on his play.

A slap hits the kid's head and he slams his face on a stool.

Marta comes running, Julian's nose is dripping blood and mucus, and his lips are red with blood.

Audrey huffs, feeling guilty for putting too much strength into her slap. "Well, he has to learn to bite his tongue!" she says, and then to the others, "Idiot or not, he pissed me off. Sometimes it's necessary."

"You can't stand him, you never could. But if you touch him again I swear..."

"What? You'll cut my throat?" Audrey laughs out loud while Jack, acting as if nothing happened is setting the table with cups, dishes and biscuits for the tea. George is smoking a cigar, and purses his lips together to blow a smoke ring, and then he speaks for his wife. "Aunt Marta, you must admit sometimes he deserves to be drowned."

Marta is cleaning the nose of Julian who is in tears and she turns her head sharply and retorts, "Julian will say the first thing that comes to him, but he's never hurt anyone. He can't even think about hurting someone. He's a thousand times better than us."

"Cousin Audrey's evil..." Julian mumbles, spitting red, "...very evil!"

"But no!" Through the French doors, Angela comes in from the garden together with Armand. "You just need to know how to take her." Audrey trembles with fury but remains silent while Angela continues, "There was a butterfly in the garden. Weird, in this season. It's not cold, but... bravo, Jack! A hot cup of tea is just the thing."

"Your milk is hot, too, Miss Angela, just the way you like it. It's in the smaller jar." Jack bows slightly. "May I pour?"

He looks around to get everybody's permission.

George comes closer, but instead of picking up his cup, he turns and leans on the table. "I say we screw our uncle. Let's make a deal. We pick three names at random, and they sign a paper stating they will share the inheritance equally with all of us."

Angela steps to the table and pours milk in her tea. She lifts the cup to her lips but stops with a smile and turns to Jack. "Would you be a dear and taste it first, Jack?"

Jack smiles. "My pleasure, Miss Angela," and takes a sip. "But in Africa we all got hardened against cyanide," he adds softly.

Angela smiles back and drinks her tea, looking at George, who's been observing the exchange. "Does this answer you, George?" she grins over the lip of her cup.

Irritated, Audrey sits at the table. "What a bitch!" she whispers, and drinks her tea.

George huffs and takes a cup of steaming tea. "Is this mine?" he asks.

Audrey shakes her head in desperation. George makes matters worse by adding, "Out of education, not of fear from poison."

"Tea makes me shit!" Julian mumbles, his tongue swollen, and goes back to playing with his wood scraps. Marta strokes his head and can't scold him. She picks up a teacup, takes a sip and puts it back on the table. She looks at George. "My brother John knew us well. Maybe he recorded that will thinking to have us listen while he was still alive. He knew and he wanted to push it down our throat."

"Throat, Aunt, you said throat!" Julian jumps up, stares with wide-open eyes and passes his small carving knife along his neck. Then he drops it on the carpet, foaming red at the mouth.

Marta puts down her cup and runs to him. "Julian, Julian... Jack, give me that spoon! If it's an epilepsy crisis..."

Armand has been stirring the abundant sugar he'd poured in his tea. He rises and comes running, holding a spoon. He bends over Julian, then opens one of the boy's eyes and laughs at him.

"What crisis? He's just playing the fool."

Julian laughs and sits up, and scoots on his ass back into his corner and his games.

Marta lightens up and goes back to her tea. "I was saying Sir John knew us well, and if he ever had us listen to that tape while he was still alive..."

"You mean nobody would have cut his throat?" Audrey asks.

"Well, it's an idea," Armand grins, and then turns to Angela.

"What if we left this zoo?"

"In a month, honey," Angela says. "In a month." And she goes back to her tea.

"I'd leave straight away," Marta says. "I'd have left yesterday, but we are under house arrest, according to Inspector Brand. And then I have to take care of Julian's interests. As the only son, he should be the only heir."

"And you being his tutor, of course," Angela leers. "But Uncle couldn't stand that freak of nature."

Marta glances at Julian, who keeps playing, making a pyramid of wood scraps, oblivious to the others, like he didn't hear.

George starts again. "I can't believe it was one of us, but anyway... if one of us... I mean, if anyone did what they did for the inheritance, they won't like being screwed over right now."

Angela picks a biscuit and nods. "And they won't share with seven, or three, or even two."

"Anyone for seconds?" Jack asks. Angela laughs. The butler shakes his head. "I meant," he says, "Anyone wants a second serving of tea?"

"You Jack," George says, "were my uncle's friend. Did you know anything about that bitch of a will?"

"No, sir. Our friendship had somehow become tarnished as we grew older." Jack places the cups back on the trolley. "And yet when I saw John with the knife sticking in his throat ... it was like they had stuck it in mine, George, sir."

"Oh, always the affectionate, faithful servant!" Audrey chants as she picks at a biscuit.

George points a biscuit at Jack standing in front of him. It's like he wants to say something, but then he just puts the biscuit in his mouth.

Angela noticed George's hesitation and comes closer. "Hiding something, brother?"

"Who? Me? No. Why?"

"Just an impression. Do you know anything about Jack we should know?"

Audrey physically puts herself between Angela and George. "As a detective, you..."

"Suck!" Julian shrills from the back of the room. Audrey opens her arms in a gesture of exasperation. "He can't understand shit, but he doesn't miss a damn word!" she says turning her back on Angela. "Let's go for a walk in the garden, love," she says to her husband. "The

34

air in this place smells like a prison cell."

George offers some resistance, but Audrey takes him, arm in arm, and drags him to the French doors. Angela watches them go out and then gets closer to Marta. She picks up another biscuit, bites into it and says, "Aunt Marta, do you know in what whorehouse of what cesspit of a town brother George picked up that countess?"

Marta does not answer. From the pocket of the black suit she's always wearing, she extracts a deck of cards, and starts laying out her tarot.

Julian comes running and sits by her side. "It never works out, Auntie! Never!"

Angela stands in front of the big portrait of her Uncle John. "I detest this horrible thing, I so wish we could take it down."

Marta looks at her but she does not reply.

CHAPTER FIVE

The Prescott mansion grounds are enormous, and only partially looked after; beyond the edges, filled with gardenias and red cranberry, there is a wide, wild area, rife with bushes of heather, thick and fully over five feet in height. Farther still there's an oak thicket, a remainder of a far away past, when all of Yorkshire was covered in woodlands.

"Pity we can't get to those oaks out there without scratching ourselves raw," says Audrey as she brushes aside a heather brush. "When everything will be mine, I'll have these bushes cut, I'll draw a walkway to those oaks, and right in the center of them I'll have a gazebo built, with hammocks." When she gets no response, she turns to her husband, standing behind her, looking at the villa. "Are you listening to me, George?"

The man does a double take, looks at his wife, at the oaks, and then goes back looking at the house. "If I don't talk, he'll do it first... and the Inspector will believe him!"

"George, what you have to say about Jack is not proof enough, and if you start the gossip-mongering, we don't know where we'll end up."

"It's proof that Jack lied. And then he's the only one with the guts to..." and he gestures with his hand across his neck. "And if he did, now he'll find a way to do us in, too, and everyone else. "

"Under the very eyes of the police?"

"Then the inheritance is lost. The only way was to do as he said, and cut a deal with the others. If in a month we're still all here, then goodbye to the money."

"If the Inspector nails the killer, maybe later we could cut a deal. Not before, don't you see?"

"That cop wouldn't know how to find paper to wipe his own ass... 'where were you at the time of the murder?' What a brilliant question!"

Audrey laughs and kisses George, who places his hands on her hips and asks, "And without Uncle's money, would you love me all the same?"

"But of course, love! But with the money would be so much better, right? You know, I was thinking we could push somebody out of the race even without killing them. Say that Aunt Marta gets scared and runs off with that half-wit. Or maybe the Inspector nicks somebody and puts them in the slammer...”

“Aunt Marta isn't scared of the devil. And I told you, I think the Inspector's a cretin. Maybe if I tell him Jack lied...”

“Do as you please, darling, but to tell that Jack lied, you'll have to admit you did too, first.”

George grins. “That's why I think I should speak first. Whoever speaks first can claim he did not lie, he just remembered later.”

Audrey weighs the words of her husband and then kisses him again. “I didn't think of that! George you're a genius!”

The man embraces her and his hands slide down to her ass. He massages her buttocks, whispering, “And now I'm thinking about something even better...” He lifts her up and wades through the heather.

Audrey laughs. “No, George,” she protests. “These brushes sting...”

But the man does not heed her, and carries Audrey bodily beyond the first row of bushes.

Sitting on the carpet in the great salon, tongue out between his teeth; Julian does not care about the saliva that dribbles down his chin. He's busy digging a hole in the crotch of a badly mangled Ken doll. He then rams home a big shaving of wood into the hole, like a gigantic phallus. He crawls over to his aunt. She's placing the tarot cards on the table, face down. She counts and turns one: it's number XIII, Death. Marta stares at the skeleton with the scythe. “You're late...” she whispers, laughing, but her eyes are veiled with tears.

Julian grabs the chair's back and leans on his aunt, holding his priapic Ken in hand. “Why are you laughing, Auntie?”

Marta turns to the boy, sees the doll with its huge penis. “What's that thing, Julian? Nobody has one like that!”

“Oh, yes, Auntie! Armand's got one, long and hard just like this.”

Marta stands, pushing the chair away so forcibly it falls over. She pulls out the Ken doll's wooden penis and then asks the boy, “Armand? Did Armand do something bad to you Julian?”

Julian looks at her, uncertain. He takes a step back. “Bad? Nnnno... What sort of bad could he do to me, Aunt Marta?”

CHAPTER SIX

W alter Brand is in the office of Superintendent Sean Money. Money is going through some papers. Then he looks up. "You tapped the cell phones, too?"

"Yes, superintendent, as per appendix B."

The super picks the last two sheets and scans them. "Journalists, caterers... don't they have any friends?"

"There's a call from the Lions Club on the house phone, and a Mary looking for Angela. But I ordered the butler not to pass any incoming calls through."

"That butler? Then we're set. Once it was enough to block the land line, but with cell phones..."

"That's progress for you."

"But maybe it's wrong, Inspector. And not progress at all. I'm talking about cell phones. If they can talk on the phone, maybe they'll say something useful."

Brand nods. "Yes. I was hoping to solve the case in twenty-four hours, and that the reading of the will would shed some light on the business. You're right, of course. It's good if they can talk."

"Sir John Prescott was an important man. We must find the killer. And heaven forbid somebody else gets killed in that house; the press will be after our blood. Did you see the tabloids this morning? They're having a field day, the bloody vultures."

"Finding an answer won't be easy Superintendent. As you can see, we have no clues. Or, better, everybody's a prospective murderer, which in the end is the same. Did you read the will transcript? Is such a filthy thing really ... legal?"

"Apart from the minimum due to his son, yes, there's no law against such a thing. The Prescotts are not a normal lot, nor was the poor deceased Sir John. Do you need any special support in your inquiry?"

"Such as?" Brand asks, simmering.

"A psychologist. Somebody able to get something solid out of those people."

"I did an update course one month ago, and they filled my head with that psychological bullshit. They want to find killers with psychology. Just send them to London for a few weeks, on the Fonsbury Park beat, by night, like I did a few years back."

"Yes, they put too much faith in their theories, but on this case perhaps they could be useful..."

The phone rings. Money answers, then hangs up.

"A call for you from the villa," he says to Brand. "Maybe something's moving. Take it in your office."

Brand stands up and exits his boss' office.

CHAPTER SEVEN

It's night and a three-quarter moon in a clear sky illuminates the grounds of Prescott House.

Bubi is barking. A police car stops in front of the gate. Inspector Walter Brand gets out and stops the two cops that are about to follow him.

"You wait here. I think he wants to see me alone."

Mortimer runs to open the gate. "Good evening, Inspector."

"Good evening. Any new visitors since yesterday?"

"Journalists, but I sent them away as per your orders."

"Good. Keep them out." Brand sees the salon lights are on. "I know the way," he says, and follows the path as Mortimer goes back to his small studio. He quickly calls the villa with an old closed circuit phone. When Brand reaches the three steps leading up to the villa, George is already there, standing by the French windows.

"Good evening, Inspector," he greets him as he opens the door. Brand comes in from the cold.

"Brr. Clear but cold weather. Good evening, Mr. Prescott."

"Can we skip the talk about the weather?" George asks, nervously. He's clearly excited.

"Oh, certainly. What do you want to talk about?"

"Let's find somewhere to sit."

George leads the way to a salon corner, and gestures for the Inspector to sit on a stuffed chair, as he takes the chair opposite. The Inspector stares at George, who is nervously opening and closing his hands. The Inspector waits.

One long minute goes by in silence, and then George erupts in a cascade of words, as if he's trying to throw them out as fast as possible. "When I told you that I retired to my room with my wife, that night, at nine o'clock, it was true, but I lied when I told you I did not get out later. When the hallway clock chimed ten o'clock, Audrey, my wife, asked me to get her a glass of water. I went to the kitchen, everything was dark, and the room was empty! Jack lied when he said he was there having a cup of tea! And coming back with the glass of water I met him, more, he slammed into me... he was running and he almost knocked the glass out of my hand!"

Brand pulls out a notebook and jots down everything George said.

"Ten o'clock, you said."

"Yes, there's an annoying grandfather clock in the hallway, striking the hours."

At the other end of the salon, Audrey enters, wearing a nightgown. "George..." She freezes as the Inspector stands up to greet her. "Oh, Inspector. I didn't know that... I'm not presentable..."

"Miss, you are always presentable. May I ask you a few questions?"

"Yes... yes, of course." Audrey pulls her nightgown closed and stares a question to her husband, who nods his approval.

"Your husband was telling me that the night of the murder you did not stay in your room..."

"Well... I did..." Audrey looks at George.

"Darling, I told him the truth," George tells her.

Brand stops him and "Would you tell me what really happened?" he asks her.

Audrey seems worried, and keeps glancing at her husband. "I can't remember precisely, but I think as soon as I was in our room I noticed there was no water bottle, and I asked George..."

"You previously declared you retired to your room at nine, right?

"Yes, more or less. Anyway I asked George if, while he was going to get some water, could he make me some tea."

George cuts in, "No, darling, you only asked for a glass of water... For tea we would have called Jack."

"Yes? But it was late..."

"Nine o'clock was too late to call the butler?" Brand presses on.

George gestures, irritated. "Darling, it was late because it was ten pm, remember?"

"Really?" Audrey tries to look naive. "It's like he says, Inspector, I... my recollections of the evening are confused."

"May I ask for some tea?" Brand says. "It's such a cold evening."

Audrey smiles and rings a small bell. "Of course, Inspector."

Jack enters and bows slightly to the Inspector. "Good evening, Inspector. Can I be of assistance?"

"The Inspector wanted some tea, Jack," Audrey says while George paces impatiently.

"Straight away, sir."

"No, let it go. Your name is Jack, right?"

"At your service Inspector. You no longer wish to have some tea?"

"Thanks, no. It was just to see if it was possible to get some tea at nine pm."

"I don't understand, sir."

"The night of the murder you said you went to the kitchen to have some tea."

"Yes. But it was ten. I never get off duty any earlier." Jack stares at the Inspector without showing any surprise.

"But apparently you were running in the corridors," Brand says.

Jack looks interrogatively at George who adds, "Yeah! You were running and you crashed into me. Why were you running, Jack?"

The butler remains silent for a moment, and then with a sorry face, "It was you, running, sir," he says. "Don't you remember?"

George loses control. "Liar!" he shouts. "You were running, Jack! And where did you come from? From Uncle John's office, that's where!"

"This is too much, George. I think my duties do not extend quite this far. I was willing to remain silent, but I can't just take the blame in your stead."

George advances menacingly and the Inspector steps between the two men.

"Calm down!"

"Inspector, you won't believe the words of a servant over a member of the family!" Audrey exclaims, glancing at the butler, who's standing at ease.

"Miss, please. Here social roles are irrelevant." He turns to Jack. "You say one thing and Mr. Prescott says the opposite. One man's word against another's. Can you give any proof of the fact that you're telling the truth?"

Jack shakes his head, and then remembers. "No. Ah, maybe yes. George was wearing a dressing gown, he was distraught, he crashed into me and to keep my balance I grabbed him and I tore away a button off his purple gown."

"Lying bastard!" George screams. "You're the killer!"

Audrey embraces her husband to stop him. "George, please!"

"Do you have that button?" the Inspector asks.

"No. I let it drop, I think. I can't remember..."

"Off course you don't have it, you liar!" George screams. Not even Audrey's embrace can placate him.

The Inspector holds up a hand and asks for silence. Then, "Can we see this dressing gown?" he asks.

"Sure, Inspector!" Sure! This way you'll know you've caught the killer! Let's go to my room!" says George triumphantly.

"What's happening? Why the shouting?" Marta is standing on the door, in her eternal black dress.

"Aunt Marta, it's him, it's Jack. He killed Uncle John!" George points at the butler who quietly shakes his head, unflinching, as his profession requires.

"Madam, I don't know what got into your nephew. You know I would have never hurt John... Sir John."

"Let's go and check this dressing gown," Brand orders.

George takes the lead and climbs up the staircase, mumbling insults at the butler. Jack lets Marta pass, and follows, last in the line.

Once in the big hallway, Julian emerges from one of the doors, amused at those people walking fast towards George and Audrey's room. He tags along.

"One, two! One, two! One, two!"

Marta hangs back and takes his hand.

"This is a grownup thing, Julian! Let's go to my room to play cards, ok?"

"Later!" the boy says, and pulls Marta along forcing her to follow the group.

George opens the door to his room, enters boldly and opens the wardrobe. The clothes, dressing gowns and overcoats fill a whole wall. George finds the purple gown and takes it off the hanger, and throws it at the Inspector.

"Here, look, Inspector, and then arrest that liar!"

The Inspector picks up the dressing gown and checks. Three buttons and three buttonholes. He looks at Jack.

"Three buttons and three buttonholes. No button missing."

Jack observes it and then spreads his arms. "What can I say, Inspector. Somebody must have sewed it back on again."

The Inspector takes a closer look at the buttons. The middle one is badly attached using white thread. It was clearly sewn by someone unskilled. "Did you sew it back, miss Audrey?" he asks, pointing at the white thread and the skewed placement of the button on the gown.

George widens his eyes and grins. "My wife couldn't sew a button to..."

"... to give you an alibi, Mr. Prescott?" The Inspector's voice is cold, professional.

Audrey takes the gown and squints at the button. She purses her lips in a kissing pout. "I don't remember," she says. "But if I did sew it on, it was ages ago."

"Yes, miss. Provided the wife can't testify against the husband, I suggest you keep your lies to a minimum."

George pulls the gown away from Audrey's hands and studies the white thread that screams it was attached by somebody that can't sew.

"George!" Audrey stomps her feet. "If you keep staring at that damn button I'll start screaming!"

George throws the dressing gown in Jack's face. The butler has kept quiet, like he was not involved in the proceedings. "You, you, fucking bastard!" You pulled it off and then reattached it in this slipshod way!"

Brand stops George. "Calm down. That button's a clue, yes, but it does not prove a murder."

George sits down on his bed, feeling empty. He shakes his head to negate reality, denying it to himself while the ineffable Jack puts the gown back on its hanger and places it back in the wardrobe.

CHAPTER EIGHT

"And you didn't nick him?"

"For a badly sewn button? Doesn't sound like enough to go to court to me."

"Yes, but in that house somebody's plotting something. Inspector, maybe you should arrest that Prescott guy, George Prescott. Give him three days in the hold, and then we see what happens."

Brand hangs up. The super might be right. But there's no reason to arrest George, three days in the slammer would be an abuse. Yet he complies with his boss and calls his assistant and orders him to prepare a detention form for George Prescott.

"We'll execute it tomorrow morning," he says and hangs up. Brand checks the time. He should go to dinner, but he's not hungry. Better a good beer at The Vic. He starts out on foot; it's only a few hundred yards. The air is cold, but still above freezing. The sky is a clear blue and the wind has cleared the air. In moments like these he misses his wife. Often she'd fix him a sandwich with some lettuce and bacon, when she knew he could not make it home. But Brand always did everything he could to get home anyway. He had been transferred to vice, and he often came home late at night.

He pulls his coat collar up. These days he tries to go home as little as possible. And then just to sleep. Edwige went in two weeks. She was forty-two and beautiful. Lung cancer, and she had never smoked in her life.

The Inspector stops at the crossroads and lights up a cigar.

CHAPTER NINE

The sun goes down and the cold wind of West Wiltshire rises. It shakes the tops of the heather bushes in the garden of the Prescott mansion. Mortimer is raking dead leaves and stops to stare at the villa. A light has gone up in one of the first floor windows. Mortimer can see Angela as she pulls the curtains closed, and behind her the shadow of a gesticulating man. The watchman drops his rake against a hedge and goes back to the entry studio where he lives. He switches on an ancient interphone that connects him to the house, and presses two switches. He sits, listening. Drowning in static, he can hear Armand's voice.

"It will be a hellish month. Whoever the killer is, they might kill again. Why don't we leave for a few weeks? We come back to go see the attorney."

Angela sits on the bed and sighs. Armand takes a gulp from the beer bottle he's holding.

"There's glasses in the bar," Angela points out.

The man shrugs impatiently and puts his beer down. *"Answer what I said: we leave for a month."*

Angela watches the pretty boy in front of her and shakes her head. *"Sometimes I think you're just a pretty face. First of all we were ordered by the police to stay at home. Just imagine leaving the city. And going away we'd leave a free hand to the killer."*

"We can deal with the cops. We go to Bexhill, to my mother's, and we stay put. What difference does it make to the cops? And that Inspector looks to me like a poor bastard, and he's not happy at all of this mess he's been saddled with."

"Don't judge people from their looks," Angela sighs again. *"You might blunder, badly."* She weighs him with her eyes as she lights up a cigarette.

Armand does not get the hint, unable to perceive it, and goes on. *"Let's get away Angela. I'll talk to the Inspector."*

"Do you know how much Uncle John's inheritance is estimated to be? Eight hundred million pounds sterling, and I believe that is a conservative estimate."

Close to his interphone, bent over to catch every word, old Mortimer cups his ear with his hand: the old gizmo is whistling and he must twist the dials to tune it in.

"I know." Mortimer catches Armand's voice coming in sharply, and also Angela's reply. *"I know you know, or you wouldn't be here."*

Bubi, the dog, barks, and Mortimer runs out: there's a pizza

46

delivery van at the gate.

A kid gets out of the van, carrying two pizza boxes. He checks the ticket sticking to the top and says, "Marta Prescott, express delivery."

Mortimer opens the gate without undoing the chain, and stretches his hand. "Give it to me."

"I deliver in person. Tip, you know."

Mortimer rummages in his pockets and drops a coin in the kid's hand. "Police orders, kid. Nobody gets in the house. Now beat it."

"But the pizzas..."

"Nobody!"

The kid relents and hands the two pizzas to Mortimer. He huffs, "Bummer. The Evening Post chick promised fifty quid for a look in the villa."

"Those people are vultures. You should know better anyway."

Mortimer shuts the gate and walks away, Bubi hot at his heels.

"But what's it like in there?" the kid calls after him.

Mortimer does not turn. He twists his arm and lifts a hand behind his back, giving him the finger. There's a diamond ring on it.

The kid doesn't notice the ring. He flips the old man back, and goes away, laughing.

Mortimer re-enters his studio and presses two switches on the intercom.

"Jack?"

"Yes, Mort, what's up?"

"Two pizzas for Miss Marta."

"Okay. Bring them up."

Pizza boxes in hand. Jack knocks at Marta's room. "Madam, the pizza."

Marta opens the door and takes the boxes in. She says nothing and shuts the door again.

Jack grins and knocks again. Marta opens the door again. Behind her, Julian is opening the boxes.

"Margherita pizza again!" he wails. "I don't like this bloody shit... they look like somebody with hemorrhoids made them..."

"Madam," Jack says, "I don't feel well, with your permission I'd like to retire."

Marta looks at him, than she nods and closes the door.

Jack climbs the stairs to the attic. He hears voices and stops to listen. He thinks it must be George, shouting something, and Audrey getting back at him. A door opens on the hallway, and Jack is quick to hide in the shadows of the staircase.

George leaves the room. "You said you remembered sewing it back," he shouts, angry. "Instead you should have said that you never reattached a button in your damn life!"

"Oh, c'mon, George, just fuck off!"

Audrey slams the door and locks it.

"What did you say?"

"Fuck off!" Audrey shouts from within. George can't believe it. Surprise replaces anger. "How long have you been using this kind of language, Audrey?"

"Since I was born, you prick!"

George opens his mouth, bedazzled. He lifts his foot to kick the door, but stops.

Angela comes out of her room, and looks at her brother. "What's up dear brother of mine?"

"Nothing. Maybe Audrey is not feeling herself. She's having her monthly, probably."

"She's been having them for thirty years, you moron. Come on, let's go to the kitchen and fix us some bacon and eggs like old times. If we keep skipping dinners, we'll never make the end of the month ourselves?" She pulls George along and he follows her, unenthusiastic but without any serious resistance.

Jack is standing in front of the attic door. He has the key out to open it, but the door is already ajar. He pushes it wide but does not enter. Inside it is dark: from the gable window a memory of twilight frames the bed, the nightstand and a small desk against the wall.

Nobody's there. Jack stretches out his hand and turns the light on. A small chandelier illuminates the attic. The bed is set, nothing's amiss. Jack steps in and locks the door behind him. He bends down to check under the bed. He opens the wardrobe by the side of the door and then checks the small bathroom in an alcove off the thick main wall of the mansion. He makes sure to look into the shower.

Now reassured, he goes to the small electric stove, to make some tea. He looks in the mirror on the wall. The skin around his mouth shows some early, thick lines. He bites his lips and wets them, to make them full like they were once. He tries to pull the skin around his eyes: here, this way it would be fine, apart from a vague Chinese folding of the eyelids. Jack gets closer to the mirror and stares himself in the eye. Here nothing's lost; his eyes are still deep and luminous like they were in his twenties. While the tea water heats up, Jack opens a drawer and takes out a photograph. It's a photo taken of him at the diamond mines in Africa. Jack is young, bronzed. His arm is around the shoulders of a heavyset man of about forty. Sir John when he was not yet a sir. Crouching on his heels right in front of them is the man whose portrait Marta wears around her neck: her husband, Arthur Burton. In the photo he's laughing, and the three men appear happy. Jack puts the photo back in the drawer, and pours the boiling water from the teapot into a cup, adding a spoonful of dried tealeaves. He sits on the bed and takes off his shoes.

There's a note on his pillow.

"Ten o'clock."

Nothing else. But to Jack it carries a lot of meaning. He looks at his watch. It's barely seven; he's got all the time he needs. He opens a drawer in his nightstand, and pulls a gun out. He checks that it's loaded, and puts it back. He drinks his hot tea standing, looking again at his reflection in the mirror. He puts down the cup and goes to the door, turns the key, and opens it. Closes it and leaves it unlocked. He undresses to take a shower. He has to bend a little not to hit his head on the showerhead. The water cascades down his shoulders, running down his muscular body, and leaving his gray curls dry.

CHAPTER TEN

In the kitchen, Angela is frying bacon and George is sitting in a chair, holding his head with a hand.

"Suddenly vulgar. She told me to fuck off! Audrey! My fairy princess!"

Angela laughs. "She's not the fairy princess you think!"

"Angela, please!"

"Big brother, I never told you, but your pretty little lady told me to fuck off an infinite number of times, and explained to me I'm a parasitic lesbian slut, a hyena waiting for the body of Uncle John."

George looks at his sister, to see if she's joking. Angela nods in confirmation. She breaks three eggs open in the frying fat, and turns the bacon, that sizzles, its greasy smell filling the air. "Smell the perfume..." Angela says, inhaling with gusto the oily steam rising from the pan. "Get me the mustard, the French one."

George opens a cupboard and brings two pots of mustard to the table.

"You're kidding me, right?"

"But no! She's been kidding you, always. The flatware, George!"

The man moves like an automaton as Angela dishes the eggs out onto a big plate in the middle of the kitchen table.

"Crackers? Like some?" Angela opens a pack of crackers that's sitting on the table and breaks one with her teeth, chewing with pleasure.

"One of them broke," Angela says, pointing at one of the poached eggs, the yellow spreading in the hot fat.

"Why three?" George asks.

"One's enough for me. I'll take the broken one. You take the whole ones."

George stops Angela's fork hand. She caresses his hand and says, "We said that when we were kids, remember?"

George nods, and serves one of the whole eggs on his sister's plate.

"It was good, then. We were so innocent."

Angela nods and dips a second cracker into the egg yolk, breaking it. George wraps a slice of bacon around his fork and eats it. He asks,

"But really Audrey said those vulgar things to you?"

Angela chews and nods.

"Why?"

Angela laughs and nearly chokes. George taps her on the back. "Because... it's true," she coughs. Tears in her eyes, she laughs and coughs again. "...and yet she was not insensitive when I touched her like this..."

Angela caresses her brother's earlobe. George turns away.

"Drop it, you're always the same. Those were childhood games Angela."

"Bon appétit!"

Marta carries the empty pizza boxes to the kitchen's garbage bin. She folds the boxes and pushes them down into the black bag. Julian follows behind her, lips bent in a disgusted grimace. He sniffs at the air and asks Angela, "Yuck! Did you fry the dead man?" He follows his query with and eerie singsong laugh.

"That's your own smell," Angela replies. She cleans up the plate with a cracker.

A cell phone rings. George rummages in his pocket, pulls out an old phone.

"It's tapped," Angela says.

"I hope not. This is Mortimer's," George replies, and then in the phone "Yes, it's me," he says. "What? Damn, when? Damn, damn, damn … Yes, thanks, yes. I'll work out something."

"He said damn, damn, damn," Julian says petulantly. "Why can he say it and I can't?"

"Because you are not a boor," Marta says to Julian while scolding George with the tired voice of habit. "You can't talk anymore without vulgarities."

But George is not listening. "They are going to arrest me! Fuck, they arrest me! Because of that damn button, because..."

"... of that slut of a wife of yours!" Angela mocks him. George turns and slaps her face, and then he runs out of the kitchen.

Angela, massaging her cheek, laughs. "Run, run," she calls after him. "You silly cuckold!"

CHAPTER ELEVEN

A thin slice of moon illuminates the garden of Prescott House. Bubi barks. He stops immediately. Through the heather shrubs, Armand comes closer and scratches the dog's head. The dog wags its tail and Mortimer peers out of the studio door.

"Ah, it's you. It's not safe for you coming here."

"And why? I'm allowed as far as the front gate..." the young man smiles.

Mortimer goes back in his studio. Armand follows him.

"News?"

"Brother and sister remembering the old times."

"Incest?" asks Armand.

Mortimer purses his lower lip and goes back to adjusting the old intercom. "Maybe. But it's old stuff. George got a call from a friend on the force, looks like they are going to arrest him."

The intercom buzzes.

"Has that thing always worked two ways?"

"With some work. Old Lord Philip did not trust his wife." Mortimer throws a pair of switches but the intercom remains silent. Then the sound of steps, someone coughing, the sound of a chair being dragged, and a door slams.

"Somebody in the salon, but nobody's speaking."

"You should upgrade to a modern video system," Armand chuckles.

"Not with the pittance you pay me, Mr. Armand."

"Don't be greedy, and most of all don't be impatient. In a month you could be very rich."

"Or very dead."

Armand closes in on Mortimer, then turns, defensively. "Maybe you know who killed the old man?"

"Alas, no. Before the murder I had no interest in listening."

"Yeah."

A voice comes from the intercom.

"Aunt Marta, can I have my Swiss army knife?"

"The idiot..." Armand whispers. Mortimer gestures for him to shut up, and turns the dial, clearing the buzz.

"Julian, love, I'm afraid you'll hurt yourself."

"No, Auntie, I want to carve a doll. I'm good, you know?"

Some noises, then nothing. The two men listen for a few minutes, and then Armand walks away from the interphone. "I'm going back in. Angela might be wondering where I am." He goes out in the garden and breaths in the cold night air. Idly, he starts towards the house. The French windows are lit up, all the others are dark, except for Jack's gable window. He starts walking again. Another window lights up, and Armand freezes. It's the window of John Prescott's office! But the room was sealed on the Inspector's orders.

Armand walks back to the studio, hastily. "Mortimer! Mortimer..." he calls out.

In the studio, the old watchman is putting on his pajamas.

"Somebody's in the old man's office! Can you listen?"

"No, the office is not wired."

Mortimer puts on his glasses and follows Armand out into the garden.

"My Lord!" the older man gasps. "It's the master's office. Didn't the cops put tape over it?"

"Yes, they did!" replies Armand, and runs to the villa.

Julian is intently carving a small figurine from a piece of wood while crouching on the carpet at Marta's feet. She's spreading her tarot cards on the table.

Armand enters the salon, looks around.

"What happened now, Armand?" Marta asks.

"Nothing. Nothing. I was looking for Angela."

"I last saw her in the kitchen."

Armand nods and runs up the staircase to the upper floor.

Marta follows his going with her eyes, then turns a card: the Magician.

Armand walks down the long hallway with the bedroom doors. He stops and tries the handle of Angela's room, but the door is locked.

He's about to knock, but changes his mind and proceeds around the corner, to Prescott's office. The door is closed but the yellow police

tape has been broken. Armand undoes his shirt. Under his left armpit he wears a holster. The gun is a Beretta 92 Fusion. He flips the safety catch and brandishes the weapon, opening the door.

Angela is sitting on her uncle's old stuffed chair, in the exact place where she found him with his throat slit open. Her feet are on the desk, and she's smoking a small cigar. She doesn't flinch as Armand enters. She looks at the gun. "Really, Armand, a Fusion!" she says. "They didn't make many of those. How very quaint."

Armand glances at the gun, feels stupid, and lowers it. "But... what are you doing here? When the Police..."

"C'mon Armand, screw the Police! Who broke the police tape? Who killed John Prescott? Who knows? That's their problem, right?"

Armand places his gun over the bar cabinet and shuts the door. "Why are you here?"

"I'm waiting for the time..." and she points at the locked safe.

"But they sequestered everything. It's empty."

"There's a secret compartment with diamonds."

"You know the combination?"

"More or less. My uncle did tell me something."

Armand hesitates, and then he cracks up laughing as he eases closer to Angela, who is now sitting up straight, her feet off the desk and her eyes intent on Armand.

"You don't need to tell me how you got him to tell you..."

"Not the way you think, you lecher..."

Angela snuggles herself closer to Armand. She pulls his shirt open and kisses his chest. Excited, the young man grabs Angela, lifts her and lays her down on the desktop, still stained by John Prescott's dried blood.

The next card Marta places on the table is the Hanged Man. The woman stares the figure of the man hanging upside down.

"Aunt Marta, have you seen Audrey?"

George's voice causes Marta to jump. She turns and looks at her nephew, standing at the salon's door.

"No."

George goes out. Marta places another card face up. It's Death again.

George knocks on the door of his room. "Audrey, open up. They are going to arrest me! Are you still angry?" He tries to open the door, but it's locked. "C'mon, I'm tired. Open the damn door!" He shakes the door but there's no answer. He huffs, irritated and says, "Screw you bitch!" before he turns to leave but some noise from the other end of the hallway catches his attention. He gets close to his uncle's office door, and finds the police tape broken. George opens the door, catching his sister, Angela and Armand engaged in vigorous act of coitus.

"Angela!" George shouts with indignation. Armand does not look up nor does he stop his rhythmic pounding of Angela. He simply says matter-of-factly, "Do you mind going away and closing the door old chap." But George can't take his eyes off his sister, who suddenly pushes Armand back and sits up.

"Audrey is right when she calls you a slut!"

Angela sits up on the desk and brushes her hair back from her eyes with a sweep of her hand. "Of course she's right. We sluts know each other on sight. Do you know how many times your sweet little wife screwed dear Uncle John on top and beneath this desk, trying to learn the safe combination? But all the poor dear got was a measly diamond ring."

"Liar! You always hated her because..."

"Why? You tell me why I hate her, George?" Angela asks, leering, and George stumbles with his words, at a loss as he looks to Armand, who is now leaning against the safe door.

"I don't know why, but..."

"Yes you know. Because I'm jealous."

Angela is still half-naked and she comes close to her brother, staring at him with wicked eyes, her irises almost oval, like a snake's. "Because you preferred that bitch over me. And now do you know where she is? She's screwing Jack. She's been fucking him for months. They set up the button thing to frame you. You're out of the race George! You hear me? Out!"

George staggers like he was physically hit. He looks at Armand for support, but the man just gestures as if to say that it was all pretty obvious. George takes a step back, sees Armand's gun and grabs for it.

Armand dives behind the desk, while Angela stands still, giving her brother a leer full of despite.

George looks down at the gun in his hand and runs out of the office.

"Stop him! He's going kill someone!" Armand shouts.

Angela hugs Armand. "Uncle said we are too many. Too many..." She kisses Armand on the mouth but he just stares at the door, eyes wide open. Finally a decision made, he detaches himself from her and starts to make a run in pursuit of George when a chime sounds in the safe.

"It's time! Now we can open it..." says Angela with a wicked smile on her lovely face.

Angela kneels down in front of the two dials of the safe and starts turning them according to a certain combination she has in her head.

CHAPTER TWELVE

Gun in hand; George climbs the steps to the attic three at a time. He throws himself against the door to Jack's room, but there's no need to crash it. The door is open and George staggers inside. Audrey is stretching, naked, over Jack's naked body. The woman cries out in ecstasy and tries to move but Jack still her gyrations, holding her close.

"Easy, babe, the cuckold's here."

Blinded by rage, George points the gun at Jack and pulls the trigger. The other man pushes Audrey in the line of fire and the bullet hits her.

"You bastard!" George roars. He jumps at Jack, who stands still, a clear target now. George points the gun, but does not pull the trigger.

"Well, George," Jack taunts him. "Why don't you shoot me? Or did you know your wife was not such a great lay, and you could find better?"

"Die, you filthy pig!" George screams, and pulls the trigger, but the hammer clicks on an empty magazine. George stands, trembling, the Beretta in his fist. Jack takes it away from him gently, as one would do with a child. He smiles.

"And now you're not one of the three, George."

Marta enters, gasping. She ran up the stairs after hearing the shot. She sees Audrey on the floor, naked, stained with blood, legs spread open, and she turns to embrace Julian who has followed her, to keep him from seeing the grisly scene. "My God, my God..." she stammers.

George almost runs her over exiting the room. He stumbles over Julian's extended leg. The kid is peeping at the body of Audrey, grinning. "Who killed the she-pig?" he asks and then cackles in his singsong laugh.

George's fist hits him squarely in the face.

Jack is calling the police. "Prescott House," he says quietly. "Tell Inspector Brand we have another dead body."

He hangs up, steps over Audrey's body and stands by Marta's side. "Pardon me, madam, if I dare. The police will be here soon. Take the young sir downstairs and clean his nose."

Marta is too dazed to answer. Only now she notices Julian is sitting on the floor, his nose bleeding. He seems to be crying, but when she bends down she sees he's laughing.

Armand's voice comes from downstairs. "What happens? What was that noise?"

He gets no answer and walks back into John Prescott's office. "It sounded like a gunshot..." he says. Angela is dialing, once again, the combination to the safe, but the door does not open. She slams her hand on the steel surface and grins. "Bravo, Uncle! In the end you did screw me..."

Armand gives her an interrogative stare.

"The code he gave me is not the right one. Let's get out of here, the house is going to be filled with cops soon."

"Why?" Armand asks. Angela stands on the tip of her toes and gives him a kiss on the cheek. "Because it was a gunshot, and I don't thing it went astray."

George runs down the stairs, kicks open the door to his room. In his wardrobe, he grabs an overcoat with a fur collar and runs again, putting it on in full stride. He pants, soaked in cold sweat, stops and goes back, enters his room again, pulls open a drawer and stuffs a handful of banknotes in his pocket. He runs downstairs and into the garden.

Mortimer is on the doorstep of his studio, but steps up and stops him. "What's happening, sir?"

George slams into him and keeps running to the gate. It's locked. He comes back to Mortimer. "Open it, you asshole!"

Mortimer stands up and "The key's are in the studio," he stammers. George shakes the bars of the gate, it does not open. Desperate, he tries to climb over it, but the headlights of an incoming car illuminate him. He stops.

"Get down, Mr. Prescott, and keep your hands up."

It's Inspector Brand, with two uniformed men.

George lets himself slide to the ground as Mortimer comes running back with the keys.

"Open up, Mortimer," Brand orders.

Mortimer complies, and stands aside.   The Inspector comes close

to George, who's pale like a ghost in the cold lights of the car. His eyes are closed and tears are running down his cheeks. His body is shaken by a spasm.

Brand holds him by an arm. "What happened, mister Prescott?"

George opens his eyes and he stares at Brand, not recognizing him. A sigh breaks his voice. "They dropped me, Inspector," he blabbers, offering his wrists.

Brand lets him go and pushes his hands down.

"Lead us in."

George nods and starts for the house, the three men behind him. His shoulders are shaking as he cries.

Everybody is waiting in the salon, and Brand looks at each one of them in turn. He pushes George forward and "Miss Audrey?" he asks.

Marta nods, drying her eyes with a handkerchief. "Yes, upstairs, Inspector. She's upstairs."

"She's a little bit dead..." Julian says, without looking up. He's playing with two toy cars on the carpet.

"I killed her, Inspector. I found her in the arms of... of that bastard!" George points at Jack, who lowers his head, sadly accepting the insult.

"You stay here. You, Mr. Prescott, make way."

The body of Audrey is still in the obscene position it was before, and the blood pouring from her chest wound covers the floor. Brand leaves George on the doorstep, between the two cops that came up after them. He crouches down by the woman and checks her pulse, her wound. He sighs and turns to the cops. "Call the department, tell them we need the medical examiner for the crime scene. You, Prescott, are under arrest.

CHAPTER THIRTEEN

Angela yawns. It's close to dawn and Brand is still questioning them. She's sitting in a half circle together with Marta, Julian who's building a house of cards on the carpet, Jack and Armand.

"So the story of the button was a set up," the Inspector says.

Jack nods. "Yes, Inspector. Audrey had long been my lover. Sir John found it out and threatened to tell George, unless..."

"Unless?"

"She became his lover."

"Go on."

"I was the one running that night, when I crashed into George. I was coming from their bedroom . . . I was distraught. Audrey had just told me that she had fought back John's... Sir John's advances, by sticking a knife in his neck."

Marta shakes and hits Julian's house of cards with her foot. The cards collapse.

"Aunt!" Julian whines, "Look what you've done! You know all you have to do is just touch a card for the house to fall down!"

Nobody pays any attention to the boy. Jack's revelation is too important.

"And so it was Miss Audrey that killed the old man," Brand murmurs. "Or at least you say it was her, and she can't talk anymore. And why the button?"

"We were desperate, sir, Audrey and me. Should George relate about the accident... so we thought about the button gimmick to make it look it was George the one running that night... We hoped there would be no need to tell the truth. Poor Audrey was just acting in self-defense, but..." Jack stops and shakes his head, momentarily succumbing to emotions. "But Audrey was willing to confess, had things got rough for George. We just hoped it would not be necessary; no court would hang George for a button. So we thought, then. But George found out about the two of us... he lost his mind and he used that gun. I think he wanted to kill me, but instead he killed his wife."

Two men carrying a stretcher come down the staircase. A white sheet covers Audrey's body. The police surgeon flows them.

"We're done," the doctor tells Brand. "Single shot, straight through the heart. The poor thing probably didn't even realize she was dead."

"Looks like we're done, too," Brand says, standing up. "Nobody leaves town before the court testimonies."

"Can we leave this house of death, Inspector?" Angela asks. Brand stares at her, perplexed, and nods.

"Yes, it seems the crime's been solved." He thinks for a moment. "It seems," he repeats.

Armand hugs Angela protectively. "Why do you say it seems, Inspector? Now that everything's been made clear."

Brand nods again, looking at the gathered family members.

"Because there are still five of you."

"Uh, for the inheritance?" Angela smiles. "We'll work out a deal, don't worry."

"Sure," Brand says. "I'm sure you will."

CHAPTER FOURTEEN

It's a cold morning. The sky is the color of dirty linen. Inspector Brand filed his report and dropped it into the still deserted superintendent's office. When the super reads it, he thinks, he'll be pissed off. Brand had been ordered to arrest George Prescott, and he gave the man the time to kill his wife. And the cocktail of sex and blood disturbs him. He goes to the bathroom, and splashes some water on his face. He looks at himself in the mirror. His unshaven stubble makes him look like a retired old man.

"I'm getting old," he tells himself. He wipes his face with a paper towel, and then looks again. "No, I'm old already."

He walks home, and then he changes his mind and stops at The Vic, the chairs still upside-down on the tables. Goes to the bar and orders a beer.

"On an empty stomach, Inspector? I can fix you a couple of eggs with bacon..."

"No, thanks. I'm not hungry."

Brand pulls out his cell phone. He keys in an SMS message while the barman places a beer in front of him.

A few minutes later, a shivering Julie comes into the pub. She goes and sits by Brand, who's already working his way through his third beer. "You usually call me at a different time..." she starts in a sexy tone, but gets serious as she stares at the Inspector's face. "Something wrong, Walter?"

"Maybe too right. I promised I'd call you as soon as I knew the name of the Prescott case murderer."

"If you solved the crime, why the long face?"

"I feel as if they mocked me."

"For starters," Julie says, "out with the name." She gets ready to note it in the memo of her cell phone.

"Audrey Prescott."

"Ah, the sexy wife. Did she 'fess up?"

"No, she died."

Julie freezes with her finger on the cell phone keyboard. She flips it closed. "Suicide?"

"No. Her husband. One shot to the heart."

"Why?"

"Found out she was screwing the butler."

"Uh. Sex and death. Upstairs and downstairs. My editor will love it. The husband also found out she was a murderess?"

"No, he didn't know."

"Who told you then?"

"Her lover. The butler."

"OK. So what's wrong?"

"I don't know. Another pint, please."

Before the barman can take the order, Julie pulls Brand off his stool. "You want to get drunk, you might as well do it at my place. You're a public officer."

Brand says nothing, and lets her drag him away.

Julie lives in a pale blue bedsitter in a big condo, blue like the Yorkshire sky on a good spring day. It's beyond the trunk road, by the river port.

She opens the door and enters. Brand follows. "You really want another beer?"

"No," Brand replies, pulling off his coat and throwing it over a chair back. He lets himself fall on the bed. Julie goes into the kitchen. "Maybe a little coffee would be better? Walter...?"

No reply: Inspector Walter Brand is snoring, loud and slow. Julie sits at her PC and starts writing her piece for the Evening Post.

A chain of murders in Prescott House: George Prescott kills wife, the body of John Prescott is the mandator.

The heirs of the peer are seven, but only three or less will have to step up at the end of the month to cash in the inheritance. Nobody gets anything otherwise. Last night, George Prescott killed his wife Audrey with a gunshot to the heart, and was arrested by Inspector Walter Brand. The man had found his wife in the arms of the butler. So, two are out, five to go. Who will be the next victim?"

The article goes on listing the rumors about the Prescott household and Armand, sitting in the kitchen, crumples the newspaper in anger.

"This bitch says I'm your gigolo."

"Angela is frying breakfast and does not turn.

63

"Why waste time reading? That kind of journalism is just mental wanking for losers. You know, I wanted to be a journalist too once, and I have a master in journalism. I did two internships too." She stirs the bacon in a rising a cloud of greasy steam. "They only wanted two things of me: that I bring them coffee, and that they could pat my ass."

Angela drops eggs and bacon in Armand's plate. He's still angry as he picks up the paper again and soothes its pages.

"But she's right about one thing. There are still five of us."

"I'll try and deal with Jack, maybe fifty thousand pounds will be enough."

"I could talk to him."

"You? No."

"Why."

"Eat your breakfast before it gets cold." Angela sits down at the table and attacks her eggs with some crackers.

"Can you please stop treating me like an asshole?" I asked why can't I go and talk to Jack."

"All right. Because Uncle John thought you were a prick, full of muscles but without any cojones. And Jack, as you know, was not a butler to my uncle, but an old buddy. They had shared adventures, debauchery and who knows what else."

"So what? That shit your uncle's dead, even if I can't see Audrey cutting his throat!"

Angela chews and nods. "Yes," she says with her mouth full. "But Jack always agreed with the old man's opinions."

Armand drops his fork in anger. Then his expression changes, and he laughs. "You also often agreed with your dear old uncle's opinions, didn't you?"

"Sometimes," Angela winks and then laughs. "And you, my sweet Armand, have some hidden qualities dear old uncle could not imagine."

Armand chuckles, picks his fork up. He swallows a mouthful of sizzling egg yolk. "And some *you* can't imagine either."

CHAPTER FIFTEEN

A copy of the evening post is on the superintendent's desk. Money is reading the article, and then looks up at Inspector Walter Brand, sitting in front of him. The Inspector is freshly shaved and well rested.

"And where did this bitch get her information?"

Brand is impassive. "Journalists are persistent, but the female of the species always know everything."

"Because they pay their informers with blow jobs?" Money asks, aggressively. He stares accusingly at Brand.

"Maybe. Never had a chance to find out," the Inspector replied quietly.

"Maybe the bitch is right," says Money slamming his hand down on the page. "There are five of them left, if only three can cash in, two more will die."

The phone rings. The superintendent picks it up and listens.

"We're coming straight away," he says and hangs up. He stands. "George Prescott tried to hang himself," he says to Brand. "He's in the jail infirmary."

Brand stands in turn. "Weird," he observes. "Cuckolds don't generally kill themselves after killing their spouse. Before, yes, sometimes."

Julian is trying to fold the newspaper to make a boat, but he can't make it work.

"Aunt, show me how to do a boat?"

Marta takes the paper and her eye falls on Julie's headline. Her eyes scan the first few paragraphs, then, "This is today's paper," she asks Julian, "Where did you get it?"

"But it's not today's! It's old! It's the old papers Mortimer gave me to play with."

"Use another one, dear. Don't move. I'll be right back, and we'll make lots of boats."

Marta stands.

Through the window of his studio, Mortimer sees her coming, and waits for her on his doorstep. The woman in black with her husband's portrait around her neck always awed him, even if Marta rarely spoke to him. Now he sees her coming with long purposeful strides, carrying a copy of the Evening Post, and he prepares to stand his ground.

"You gave today's paper to that poor creature?"

Mortimer's eyes widen in surprise. Marta throws the paper in his face. Mortimer picks it up and looks at it.

"Who brought this rag here?" she fumes.

"I'm a subscriber, madam, but I think my copy is still on my bed. Just a minute." Soon Mortimer is back, carrying another copy of the paper. "See? This is my copy."

"You did not give Julian some papers?"

"Yes. Three days ago. Old newspapers. Your nephew likes to cut them up. Should I not be giving them to him?"

Marta does not answer. She turns on her heels and walks back to the house, slapping her thigh with the folded newspaper.

Pale, the oxygen line in his nostrils and his neck bandaged, George is perfectly clear headed. The nurse lets Money and Brand in. George glances at the Inspector and pulls the cannula from his nose.

"They dropped me, Inspector! They cut me out. I did not mean to shoot my wife, but that bastard Jack, the fucking count of Volleroy screwed me royally! The bastard used Audrey's body as a shield, and the gun had a single shot."

The nurse forces George to put the nasal cannula back into his nose.

"Keep calm, Mr. Prescott. I'm here with superintendent Money to listen to your side of the story. Tell us everything ... but keep calm."

"Was it your gun?" asks Money.

George studies him with a long look. "No. I think it belongs to Armand, that other pig living in the house."

"And why you were carrying it?" Money insists.

George gets agitated, grimaces, but then relents. "I caught that pig screwing my sister, and I picked up the gun, there..."

"Am I mistaken, or isn't your sister engaged to the young man?" Brand says.

"Alas, yes."

"And you wanted to shoot your sister's boyfriend because..."

"They were doing it on Uncle John's desk!"

Brand can't hold back a smile at the answer, but Money looks at him, annoyed.

"Didn't you seal the crime scene, Inspector?"

"Of course I did, the door was taped was per regulation but I fear these people don't give a damn about the law or police seals."

The superintendent turns back to George.

"You took the gun but instead of shooting your sister's beau, you killed your wife?"

Again George pulls the oxygen line from his nose, and tries to get up. The nurse pushes him back.

"Maybe you should stop this," the nurse says. "He's getting too agitated, and he has a light pulmonary edema."

"Just one last question," Money says. "Mr. Prescott, did you know your uncle, Sir John, was murdered by your wife?"

George stares, then he opens his mouth, and then he throws his covers off and tries to stand up. The nurse is holding him as he starts screaming.

"What the hell are you saying? You asshole! The murderer's that bastard Jack!"

Two other nurses rush in, to try and calm George down. One of them gives him a tranquilizer injection. Money and Brand are escorted outside.

A police car is waiting outside the jail's main gate, but Money points at the sidewalk along the prison wall.

"A little walk, Inspector?"

"Sure. May I smoke?"

"Granted."

"You want one? Italian cigars. Strong but tasty."

"No. I quit. What do you think?"

"About George Prescott?"

"Yes, and about all of this bloody mess. Yesterday the mayor called to congratulate me: case solved, murderer dead. Perfect."

"If there's something that's far from perfect, it's this nest of vipers, Superintendent."

"What do you suggest, Inspector?"

"Even if I know you won't like it, a press conference, in which we'll explain that the wife of Sir John's nephew was accused by the servants, but only after her death, and we are checking the facts."

"The mayor won't like it either. He'll think we're backing up."

"We are backing up, but what if somebody else dies in that insane asylum? It can get far nastier than it is right now."

The superintendent gestures for the car following them to drive up and the two men get in.

CHAPTER SIXTEEN

Angela presses the start button on a small tape recorder, and a male voice speaks. It is Jack's voice.

"But do you know he spent two years in the Foreign Legion to sidestep a charge of murder?"

"Who, Armand?" says Angela's voice.

"Yes, your sweet lover is a cold-blooded killer, or so the prosecution said."

"C'mon, Jack, this one you made up."

"Ask him, Angela. You ask him. Maybe when he fucks you he might hold your throat a little too tight."

"Stop it. You're being ignoble."

"Ignoble? Oh no, I am noble. It's all of you who are ignoble..."

A short laugh echoes on tape.

"Oh, yes... your grace the count!" Angela voice is full of irony. *"And what does the count suggest, then?"*

"Kill him."

"You can't do the Audrey-George game again, two birds with one stone. It won't work a second time. And you forget a point."

"And that is?"

"I love Armand and I can't wait to cash in my share of inheritance so we can go party in Hawaii. We've already set our sights on a bungalow in Molokai. Just a green golf lawn in the front and then miles of pink sand beach, never touched by human feet."

"You might fulfill your romantic dream with someone else. What about me? Experience counts for something..."

"Hands off, you pig!"

"I have some African drugs that will scramble his brains, and you can have him sign anything. Make him write that it was him who killed the old man, and then we'll watch him commit suicide."

"You're a scoundrel and a criminal just like Sir John. Marta always suspected you two killed her husband off to avoid sharing the diamond mines."

"Why split when one can take everything?"

"Enough! I don't know why I'm standing here listening to you..."

There's a sound of steps, and then a male voice shouting, *"If you don't do it I'll put a bullet in his damn head!"*

"And I will call the police."

"No, my pretty one. You won't call anyone. You will have committed suicide, dragged down by the guilt of cutting your uncle's throat."

There's a sound of struggle, then Angela's strangled voice. *"Help! What...! You're crazy! Hel..."*

Then there's a thump and the sound of a body being dragged on the floor, and the recording stops.

Angela looks at Mortimer. "Is this believable? Will he think it's Jack talking?"

"Yes, I'll pretend it's live from your room."

"Fine, Mortimer. If this works out, you'll get one hundred thousand."

"It will work, Miss Angela. It will." Mortimer smiles as he sees her to the door. "May I ask a question?"

Angela stops and nods.

"Whose voice is that man?"

Angela smiles, contracts her diaphragm and replies in a deep, grumbling male voice. "It's my masculine half, Mortimer!"

Surprised and delighted, Mortimer bows. "Great performance, miss."

"Thank you." Angela smiles, does a pirouette and exits after checking nobody's watching from the house windows.

Mortimer's eyes follow her going and he smiles to himself saying, "Betting on many horses makes one's winning likelier."

CHAPTER SEVENTEEN

Julie is in Brand's bed and is browsing the news. She throws the newspaper to the ground and shouts to be heard over the sound of the shower. "I may as well stop warming up your bed. Nothing more's happening."

Walter comes out of the bathroom, a towel wrapped around his hips, drying his hair with another towel. "What day is it?" he asks.

"If we screwed for more than twenty-four hours, it should be March the 17th, a Thursday..." she checks the alarm clock on the nightstand. "Nine-twenty. Wow! At the Post they'll be wondering what happened to me!"

"Maybe they know!" Brand laughs. "Tomorrow is the 18th, the day of reckoning for the Prescott family heirs." He walks to the calendar on the wall and taps his finger on the number eighteen, circled in red. "Tomorrow we'll see who gets John Prescott's money."

Julie gets up and walks to the bathroom, yawning. "They will strike a deal and let bygone the bygones. Case closed, my dear Inspector."

The cell phone rings in Brand's jacket pocket and he fumbles to get to it. "Hello? Yes, Inspector Walter Brand. Ah, fine. I'll be there in a few minutes."

Superintendent Money spreads a few photographs on the table similar to the one used in John Prescott's murder, and then shows Brand the murder weapon with the crude 'A' etched on the wooden handle.

"We've received a reply from South Africa. It's a Boer knife, they say Kruger himself always carried one on his belt."

Brand eyes the photo. "Anything on Burton's murder?"

"Arthur Burton was found with his throat cut in his house. The murder weapon was never found. The case was archived as a robber/murder by an unknown assailant."

Brand reads the report and his eyes light up.

"A for Arthur!" Brand points his finger at the dagger in the transparent bag. "This is the murder weapon and somebody used it to avenge Burton's murder."

"The only one who was in South Africa with Prescott is that weird sort of butler. The one accusing George Prescott, what's his name..." and he starts rummaging through the papers.

"Jack de Villeroy, the butler," Brand says. "But the one with a motive for the murder is not him. It's the widow, Marta Prescott Burton!"

CHAPTER EIGHTEEN

The Sun is stained gray and is starting its downward course above Prescott house. Two police cars stop in front of the gate. A honk of the horn brings Mortimer to the gate. The man opens the gate. "Inspector Brand! What's happened?"

"What has happened here, Mortimer."

"Nothing, Inspector. Ever since we've learned who killed Sir John, nothing. It's all over, isn't it?"

"Maybe? Is everyone home?"

"No, Miss Angela and Mr. Armand are out shopping."

"Is Miss Marta home?"

"Yes."

"Fine. I'm here to ask her some questions."

Mortimer throws the gate open and steps aside. The Inspector gestures for two of his men to follow him.

"If those that are out come back," he says the other cops, "send them to me straight away."

Marta is in the salon with her tarot. She stares at Jack as he ushers the Inspector and the uniformed policemen into the salon. She does not stand. She gestures for Jack to leave and the butler leaves the room.

The two cops remain by the French doors, and Brand comes closer to Marta. Only now he sees Julian sitting at the woman's feet, partially hidden by her ample black skirt. He's building a house of cards.

"What more do you need to know, Inspector"

"May I please sit?"

"Why this visit? I thought the case closed, and you have no right to come back and bother us."

"May I please sit? Brand asks again. Marta waves at him. The Inspector drags a chair to the table and he bends to observe the locket the woman wears around her neck.

"Your husband, Arthur Burton, right?"

Marta nods and places another tarot card on the table. She nervously glances at the card. Brand looks at the tarot Marta placed by the others. It's a picture of a black goat with long horns.

"I'm no expert but I don't recall such a card among the tarots," the

73

Inspector says. Marta looks at him, really seeing him for the first time.

"These are Crowley tarots. They reveal the secrets of the book of the Egyptian god Toth."

"What does the goat represent?"

"Evil. Are you here to discuss tarots, Inspector?"

"No, I came to ask if you killed your brother to avenge your husband, who was killed with the same knife twenty odd years ago in South Africa, and why you waited so long."

Marta does not react. She just places another tarot on the table. "Are you accusing me, Inspector?"

"No, just a curiosity. The killer of your husband was never identified, was he?"

"No."

"And his knife had an A etched on the handle?"

Marta lays down the tarot deck.

"I don't know, Inspector. If you are really so curious, here's the story: when I left for South Africa I had only been married for a few months and my brother John had some friends there. We had a difficult time putting together the money for the trip. Arthur was a geologist and he was lucky enough to find a kimberlitic chimney fill, in other words a diamond bed. But one night somebody entered our house and killed my poor Arthur."

"By cutting his throat?"

Marta nods, affected by the memories.

Brand sighs. "Miss Marta, on the murder weapon, the one with the A there's also your fingerprints, but I have already told you that, didn't I?"

Marta nods. "Yes, Julian found it rummaging around in the attic. There is a chest filled with old stuff I don't care to see anymore."

Brand shifts to look at Julian, who does not seem to be following the discussion. He's focused, his tongue out, on placing the last card on top of his many-storied house of cards. He hesitates, tries, the house wavers.

"May I try, Julian? I was good when I was a young..."

Julian lifts his eyes to stare at the Inspector, then hands him the last card for the house. Brand kneels on the carpet and puts the card in its place without causing the house to collapse.

Julian claps his hands like a child, then with a nasty grin pulls out one of the bottom cards, and the house collapses. The kid holds the card in his hand.

"This is the fun part... ehehehehe... pull out a card and the house falls down..."

"You are a philosopher, Julian. One builds a house of hypotheses but a single piece of wrong information and poof! Everything falls apart. Was it you, the one who found the knife with the A on its handle."

Julian does not reply. He starts building another house of cards. Marta strokes the boy's head.

"Don't worry Julian, you did nothing wrong. You can answer the Inspector."

"Oh, Inspector! Are you back for a family reunion?" Angela walks in, wearing a fur coat. Armand, is behind her loaded with bags and packages.

"Good evening," Brand stands up. "We were reminiscing, with your aunt, about the good old times in Africa."

"I was just a child and I have few memories, faint memories of that country. But please, go on. Do you need anything, Aunt Marta?"

Julian finally responds to the Inspector's query. "Yes, I found it in the attic... it's a bad place, the attic, filled with spiders and dust." Julian looks up from his house of cards, and speaks haltingly. "I found it but she took it... she's evil..."

"Who's she?" Brand asks.

Julian looks up and points at Angela. Brand turns to look at the young woman, who huffs and shakes her head. "I'll just go and put my parcels. Do you mind? Come, Armand."

"Just one question, miss. Why did you find that knife with an etched A so interesting?"

"The A? I didn't notice any A. I took that big knife away from this idiot. I was worried he might hurt himself or worse, somebody else. Let's go, Armand." This time her words are a peremptory order. Angela goes up the staircase, and Armand follows, nodding as he follows in a quiet salutation to the Inspector.

As they go upstairs, Armand gets closer to Angela. "If you know something," he whispers, "it's high time you shard it with me."

She gives him a commiserating look in response.

Brand turns again to look at Marta, as she starts again placing her cards on the table. "But you did notice that A, didn't you? That meant it was your husband's knife. It meant..."

"Inspector, if you are accusing me of murder, you should arrest me. "

"After your husband's death, who got the diamond mine?"

"My brother John, he was the only surviving partner."

"Killing off the competition is a family tradition?"

Marta drops the cards and stands stiffly.

"You can arrest me, if you want, but you will not insult my family."

Brand nods and sighs. "I beg your pardon, madam, and right now I can't arrest you. But think about it. Between now and tomorrow, something unpleasant might happen."

Julian is whining. "Aunt, I shitted myself... It's this Inspector man who makes me shit!"

Armand comes down the staircase, two steps at a time. "Will you leave this fucking family be Inspector?"

The two cops take a step forward, but Brand stands up and stops them with a short gesture.

"You can go freely as you please Armand," Brand says. "You are no longer detained here. "

"That's our fucking business, right Inspector?"

Brand nods. "Yes, it's your fucking business."

CHAPTER NINETEEN

The sky has clouded over. An early dusk falls on the garden. An iron gray thunderhead rises over the house, shaped like an anvil. The wind blows in gusts, shaking the heather.

Mortimer runs to open the gate and let Brand and his two men, out, pushed by the wind that blows dust devils onto their path.

"It's going to be a bad night, Inspector."

Brand turns and stares back at the house. The salon windows are lit up, and Jack's gable window lets some light out. The house seems to stare back at the Inspector through dark, opaque windows. Brand feels suddenly uneasy.

The Inspector says goodbye to Mortimer and hastily gets in the car. The two men follow him. The car leaves and Mortimer locks the gate. He stops, faces the wind, and stares at the old house. From a pocket he extracts a pair of opera glasses and explores the face of the house. He lingers on Angela's darkened window.

Mortimer heads back in the studio and fires up his spying intercom. He pushes the buttons for Angela's room. He can hear a faint whispering, and as much as Mortimer raises the volume, the words remain impossible to understand.

In the dark, Angela is whispering to Armand.

"Now I'll go and have a talk with him. You keep this."

She hands Armand a gun with a mother of pearl grip. "I don't want to do something stupid."

"Angela," Armand breathes, embracing her. "Let me do it."

"No, he won't do anything to me. With you I don't know. Stay here, keep the lights out and wait."

Angela leaves the room. Armand listens to her departing steps growing ever fainter, and then he closes the door, takes a flashlight and goes to the window. He winks the light twice. The same signal arrives as a response from the studio at the front gate. Armand then puts Angela's gun in his pocket, puts on a leather jacket and goes out in the corridor.

The rain drums on the skylight glass, and a series of short flashes is followed by overlapping thunderclaps, like the continuous mumbling of a phlegmy old man.

The house is silent, and far away, the voice of Julian whimpers in the salon. "I won't cut myself, Aunt, I'm good with a knife, Aunt... Aunt...Aunt..."

"All right, love, but be careful..." Marta replies.

A louder sound of thunder shakes the house and Julian's voice becomes frightened. "I'm scared, I'm scared, I'm scared!"

"I'm here with you, darling. Come now, it's just a thunderstorm."

Armand listens to the voices and does not go down along the main staircase; he goes to the other end of the hallway and takes the service stairs.

The garden is dark and the rain falls straight and relentless, like it will never stop.

Armand pulls his jacket over his head and runs to the studio, followed by a thunderclap that sounds like the rattle of a dying animal. Bubi starts barking angrily in response. Mortimer opens the door and Armand enters and takes the wet jacket off.

"Well?" he asks excitedly. Mortimer gestures for him to be quiet and turns the dial of the interphone.

The voices are clear. It's the recorded voice of Angela, playing two parts.

"But do you know he spent two years in the Foreign Legion to sidestep a charge of murder?"

"Who, Armand?" this is Angela's voice.

"Yes, your sweet lover's a killer, or so the prosecution said."

Mortimer glances at Armand. "I wonder who gave the information to the bastard..." the young man whispers. Meanwhile, the voices of Angela and supposedly of Jack go on.

"C'mon, Jack, this one you made up."

"Ask him, Angela. You ask him. Maybe when he fucks you he might hold your throat a little too hard."

"Stop it. You're ignoble."

"Ignoble? Oh no, I am noble. You all are ignoble..."

A short male laugh echoes on tape.

"Oh, yes... your grace the count!" Angela is ironic. "And what does the count suggest, then?"

"Kill him."

"You can't do the Audrey-George game again, two birds with a stone. It won't work again. And you forget a point."

"And that is…?"

"I love Armand and I can't wait to cash in my share of inheritance and go party with him in Hawaii. We already set our sights on a bungalow in Molokai. Just a green golf lawn in the front and then miles of pink sand beach, never touched by human feet."

"You might fulfill your romantic dream with someone else. What about me? Experience counts for something..."

"Hands off, you pig!"

Armand is becoming furious. Mortimer eyes him with an amused smile, this muscle-bound but brain-challenged young man is falling into the trap like a blind chipmunk. He does not know the voices are coming from a small recorder connected to the interphone.

In Jack's attic the scene is completely different.

Angela is scared. She runs to the bathroom tap and lets water run. Then she comes back to Jack and whispers in his ear that Armand is in cahoots with Mortimer, and Mortimer can eavesdrop on any conversation in the house.

The butler looks at her quizzically. "Yes, I know," he says. "John knew and never had the thing pulled out. Sometimes he had fun listening in on you in your bedroom."

Angela trembles and gestures for him to lower his voice.

"Since when are you afraid of anything?" Jack whispers. "I think you'd have had no problem goring your uncle."

"Think what you will but Armand is not what he seems. He's a killer and he avoided jail by joining the Foreign Legion. He's set to swallow the whole inheritance. He said he'll share it with me, but I

don't believe him anymore. He's planning something, to kill us all and get away with it. I don't know what he…"

"We all have a plan."

Angela hugs Jack. "You saw me grow up, Jack. You were a friend of my uncle, you were with him in Africa... it's just right for you to get a share, but Armand… if he pretended he loved me just to…" she gasps.

Jack is not moved. He grabs Angela by the shoulders and pushes her down on her knees. He undoes his trousers.

"Give me a solid proof you're on my side," he grins.

In Mortimer's studio, Armand listens to the end of the recording:

"Why split when one can take everything?"
"Enough! I don't know why I'm standing here listening to you..."

There's a sound of steps, and then a male voice shouting, *"If you don't do it I'll put a bullet in his head!"*

"And I will call the police."

"No, my sweet. You won't call anyone. You've just committed suicide, dragged down by the guilt of cutting your uncle's throat."

There's a sound of struggle, then Angela's strangled voice.

"Help! What...! You're crazy! Hel..."

Then there's a thump and the sound of a body being dragged on the floor, and the recording stops.

Armand jumps.

"He's killing her... did you hear?"

Mortimer looks at him trying to look aghast, but he only half-succeeds. Armand does not care anyway, he's intent listening to the interphone. The machine is silent.

"Damn!" he curses, and runs out under the rain.

Mortimer switches the recorder off, with a satisfied grin.

CHAPTER TWENTY

The thunderstorm has turned into a virtual hurricane and the wind flattens the heather. Fiery lightning crisscrosses the sky and the thunder roars, deafening.

Crouching at Marta's feet as she studies her tarot, Julian is etching something on his wood scraps. A thunder like the crack of a cannon scares Julian and he grabs his aunt's legs. Marta bends down to hug him and her eyes catch the wood scraps the boy is playing with. Marta feels a chill. On each wood piece Julian has etched an A, a crudely drawn letter A like the one on the handle of the knife used to cut John Prescott's throat.

She stammers. "Julian... what are you doing...?"

Julian gives her a childish smile. "I etch, Aunt, etch. Do you like it?" and shows her one of the pieces of wood with the etched A.

Marta feels faint.

"But... why an A?" Then in a surge of rage she shakes him. "Why an A, that A?"

Julian whines. "Aunt, you're hurting me. I'm good at making them. Angela, too, when she saw them asked me to etch one on the handle of a knife..."

Marta's heart skips a beat. She places a hand on her chest and leans back heavily in her chair.

"Aunt! What's wrong, Aunt Marta?"

Marta keeps her eyes closed, pale and drawn, but she moves a hand to quiet the boy.

Suddenly there is a loud clap of thunder and a flash of lightning and the power goes off in the entire house. Julian screams in fear, and once again hugs his aunt's legs.

Soaking wet, distraught, Angela's gun in hand, Armand is in the dark on the service stairs. He stops, listening to the sounds of the house, but the raging thunderstorm smothers any other noise. He comes into the main hallway. He moves cautiously, holding the gun at the ready, stopping when a flash of lightning shines through the overhead skylight.

The door to Angela's room is ajar. Armand gets close and listens.

A door slams rhythmically somewhere, and the rain is pouring even harder than before. He pushes the door open with the barrel of the gun, ready for anything but not for what he sees in the light of a flash. Hanging by the throat from the hook of the chandelier, the body of Angela is still and lifeless, on the other side of the bed, wet gusts of wind blow through the open window soaking her nightgown. Armand stares at the body, and takes a step forward. A sound behind him makes him turn.

"What did you do to her, you bastard?" Jack shouts from the doorway, holding a gun.

Armand shoots him. Jack, hit squarely in the chest, staggers backward. The scream from Marta, as she comes running down the hallway, sounds like a banshee's premonition of death.

"Jaaaaack!"

In his last act before dying, Jack pulls the trigger and Armand is hit between the eyes. He crashes on the ground like a puppet whose strings have been cut.

Marta hugs Jack as he dies. The look of his face is sparked with irony as he says, "Angela won..." Marta can't hold up the butler's dead weight and the man slips to the ground lifeless.

The power comes back as suddenly as it went out. The lights in the hallway and a lamp in Angela's room light back up.

Marta walks into the bedroom.

The hanging woman opens her eyes, smiles at Marta and lifts her arms to the rope around her neck. In one hand she holds a knife, and starts cutting the rope.

Marta walks around the hanging body of Angela, who is actually standing on a black stool. The old aunt's gesture is simple, definitive: she kicks the stool out from under her niece. Angela hangs in the air, kicking, the rope strangling her. She opens her mouth, tries to cut the rope, but the noose is too tight and she can't make it.

Marta stands, impassive, looking at Angela. She doesn't answer the unasked question that wanes in Angela's eyes as life flees.

"Why?"

CHAPTER TWENTY-ONE

She looks like a ghost: a pale stain hanging over something black and dripping rain, walking to Mortimer's small studio near the front fate of the old mansion. It's Marta. Slow, short steps, eyes half closed with tears that pour down her cheeks and mix with the raindrops.

Mortimer looks at her as she advances towards him, her movements impossibly slow. He swallows his fear and goes to her, carrying an umbrella.

"Madam! What happened, Madam?"

Marta stares at him briefly, the look of a mistress to her servant.

"Call the police, Mortimer, and fix me some tea."

Julie and Brand are making love. On the nightstand, the phone rings, and then the cell phone chirps in the breast pocket of the jacket lying on a chair. Close to peaking, Brand does not want to stop right now. But Julie's cell phone rings too, on the other side of the bed. She stretches a hand out and picks it up.

"Walter, please. It's my boss."

Meanwhile, Brand's phone, that had stopped ringing, starts again. Any romantic atmosphere is now vanished. Brand gets up, throwing off the covers.

"What the hell...? Hello! What's going on, world war three?" Eh? Ah! Shit! I'm coming straight away." He turns to Julie. "I'm sorry, but I have to..." but he stops because she's already up dressing, as fast as she can.

"They told me too, my boss. We need to hurry Walter."

"Yes, but you run your way, and I run mine!" Julie slips her shoes on and runs out of the door without answering.

Brand sits on the bed to put on his shoes. "No haste. It's not like someone's dying," he mumbles. "They're all dead already."

The thunderclouds open and a clear full moon illuminates the garden.

Julian with his wood scraps in hand walks cautiously through the hallway. He sees Jack's body in front of Angela's door. He brushes next to the wall as he peeks into the bedroom. Armand's body is just beyond the door and Angela, hanging from the chandelier hook, swings to and fro in the night wind, her clothing drenched from the rain still coming in through the open window.

Julian covers his eyes with a hand, and then he opens them again and takes another step. He ignores the two dead men; he stares at Angela, her face blue, a span of tongue hanging out. Julian sticks out his tongue at her.

Mortimer pours more tea into Marta's cup, but she signals she wants no more. Inspector Walter Brand is sitting in front of her, as is superintendent Money. Beyond the door, in the ashen moonlight, more cops wait patiently on orders from their superiors.

"When my niece Angela brought me that knife, with that A etched in the handle, that my nephew Julian had found in a box in the attic, I was sure my Arthur had been killed by my brother John to steal the mine. I took the knife and confronted my brother. He did not deny it, neither did he confess. He mocked me, and I was mad with fury, so I stabbed him in the neck. You had guessed right, Inspector. What nobody could imagine is, the knife's a fake. My niece Angela asked Julian, the poor innocent thing, to etch that A on the knife, to push me, to… to make me do what I did. She wanted to be the only one to inherit the fortune and she nearly got away with it. But Julian told me the truth. And this is it."

Money stands up and gestures to Brand. "Have her taken away, no need for handcuffs. There are three dead bodies in the house. You know, Inspector, we failed. We failed badly."

Money goes away with his officers. Brand offers his arm to Marta and she, holding the locket in one hand, walks slowly to the police cars waiting outside of the gate.

Before she gets in the car, Marta turns to Brand.

"Inspector, go and find Julian, and promise me one thing: mind my poor nephew. He inherited a fortune but he can't manage it. See that he finds a good guardian and a good institution."

Brand promises, shuts the car door as soon as Marta's arranged herself on the seat, and then he walks back to the house.

The sky is clearing in the east, the moon becoming pale. The bruised dawn turns pink as it tries to defeat the night and a foggy humidity veils everything.

From the heather brushes Julie appears, carrying a camera. Brand looks at her and huffs. "You want to get me fired." Then he turns to the studio and the cars speeding away, and links his arms with her. "But who cares? Let's go. I won't get a career advance because of this damn business, anyway."

Julian stands in front of the portrait of John Prescott. He looks up with smiling, happy eyes. "Father," he says, "you always told me I was an idiot. Everybody else called me an idiot too, always. It's true I etched that A in the knife's handle, but Angela did not know it... ehhh, father, she also used to call me idiot..." And then he cackles in a weird singsong manner that ends in a low rasp.

Open-mouthed, standing on the doorstep of the salon, Walter Brand and Julie heard everything the mentally challenged boy had just said. They stand dumbstruck, like wax figures.

CHAPTER TWENTY-TWO

Nice heads of foam rise in the golden-colored beer just poured into the two glasses sitting on the table of The Vic. A waiter is pouring theatrically from a big pewter flagon.

Brand holds his glass up in a toast.

"To us poor shmucks. I can't arrest a retarded boy because he etched an A on a knife."

"Cheer up: I can't publish a story claiming the heir of the Prescott fortune is the instigator of a string of killings. His lawyers would have my skin."

"Then here's to the heir of Sir John Prescott!"

Julie clicks her glass against Brand's, and smiles. "The loser gets it all!"

Brand grimaces, and clicks his glass against Julie's.

FINE

Ernesto Gastaldi (Born September 10, 1934) is an Italian author, screenwriter, and director.. He has published a dozen books, mostly thriller, science fiction and humor. He is one of the few Italian authors to be published under his own name in an American magazine, *The Magazine of Fantasy and Science Fiction* in 1965, with his story *The End of Eternity* (translated into English by Harry Harrison.)

He has written more than 100 films, starring some of the greatest actors in the world including Sophia Loren, Marcello Mastroianni, Henry Fonda, Anthony Quinn, Telly Savalas, Carroll Baker, Barbara Steele, Terence Hill, Budd Spencer, Jack Palance, James Mason, Steve McQueen, Van Johnson, Daliah Lahvi, Pamela Tiffin, Lee VanCleef, Jean-Louis Trintignant, James Coburn, Mel Ferrer, Glenn Ford, Giancarlo Giannini, Robert DeNiro and many others.

His scripts have been directed and produced by well-known directors such as Sergio Leone, Tonino Valerii, Mario Bava, Riccardo Freda, Mario Camerini, Lucio Fulci, Damiano Damiani, and Sergio Leone among many others. Gastaldi ahs also directed six films including one of the fist and greatest giallo films of all time, Libido in 1965 starring his wife, Mara Maryl.

During that period he became one of the most important and prolific writers of peplum, giallo, spaghetti western and horror films. Among the best-known titles The Whip and the Body, Days of Wrath, My Name is Nobody, The Grand Duel, The Case of the Bloody Iris, and Once Upon a Time in America. Many of his western and giallo films have achieved a cult status around the world.

Since 1955 he's lived in Rome, where he married the actress Mara Maryl. He is the father of three children, born in 1961, 1966, and 1974.

Davide Mana was born in Turin, Italy, in 1967.

A geologist and micropaleontologist, he holds a PhD in Earth Sciences and a master in Communication of Science. He has been a researcher and lecturer, and a teacher.

A long-time fantasy and science fiction reader, Davide currently lives in the hill country of the Asti Province (Northwestern Italy); he is a writer of both fiction and non fiction, a translator and a game designer; a hybrid author, his works have been traditionally published both in Italy and in the United States, and he's a member of the Horror Writers Association.

A very mediocre jazz flutist, in his spare time Davide listens to old records, cooks and reads. He is a MOOC enthusiast, usually following four or five online university courses per year.

He blogs about adventure stories, old movies and other exotic oddities on a blog called Karavansara (karavansara.wordpress.com).

Raven's Head Press

Brings you some cool gothic horror